Tell Me Another Story

By
Carolyn Sherwin Bailey

Tell Me Another Story

THE HOME

THE TREASURE IN THE HOUSE

Once upon a time there was a little Princess, and when she was ten years old they gave her a wonderful birthday party. There were musicians, and roses in all the rooms, and strawberry ice cream, and cakes with pink icing. Every one brought gifts.

The King, her father, gave the Princess a white pony with a long tail, and a blue and silver harness. The Queen, her mother, gave the Princess a little gold tea set for her dolls. There were other beautiful gifts; a ring with a sparkling stone set in it, and a dozen or so new silk dresses, and a nightingale in a gold cage; but every one waited to see what the gift of the Princess' fairy-godmother would be.

She was late coming to the party. One never knew just how she would come, on wings, or on a broomstick. This time she came walking, and dressed in a short red gown and a white apron. Her kind eyes twinkled as she gave her gift to the Princess.

Such a strange gift as it was, only a tiny black key!

"This will unlock a little house at the end of the garden which is my birthday gift to you," the fairy-godmother of the Princess said. "In the little house you will find a treasure." And then, as suddenly as she had come, the fairy-godmother was gone, wearing one of her surprise smiles on her lips.

Every one wondered about the house, and some of the guests went to the end of the garden to look at it. All they saw, though, was a tiny thatched cottage, very neat, but not at all fine. So they turned up their noses and went back to the castle.

"A very poor present indeed!" they said.

The little Princess put the key in the silk bag that hung at her side and then forgot all about it. Not until late in the afternoon did she go to the end of the garden.

The little house made her curious, because it was so different from the castle. The castle had great, coloured windows, but the little house had tiny ones with crimson geraniums on the ledges and plain white curtains.

She opened the door and went inside. The castle had many rooms, large and lonely, but the little house had one room, small and very cozy. There was a chimney and a fireplace where a bright little fire sparkled and danced and chuckled to itself. A tea kettle hung over the hob and it was singing, as the water bubbled, the merriest song that the little Princess had ever heard. The table was set for tea. It was a very plain tea, only white bread and butter, and honey, and milk; but it made the Princess hungry to look at it. In front of the fire stood a straight-backed chair and a little spinning wheel.

The Princess sat down to her tea. How pleasant the little house was, she thought, and how unusually hungry she was!

At tea, in the castle, she often was not hungry and asked for food that was not good for her, roasted peacock, and almond cakes, and plum pudding. But here, in her own little house, she found that nothing was quite so good as bread and butter, and her milk tasted as sweet as the honey.

After tea the Princess sat down in the straightest chair, and although she had never in her life touched a spinning wheel before, she began to spin. Whirr, whirr, the wheel turned and sang, as fine white thread grew from the bunch of linen floss. The fire danced, and the tea kettle sang, and the spinning wheel whirred merrily. It was so pleasant to have had such a nice tea and to be working in her own little house that the Princess began to sing too. She sang like a bird, and she had never known before that she could sing.

"I heard you singing, and I stopped."

The Princess turned and she saw a little boy of her own age standing in the room. He had a very pleasant face, but he was dressed in ragged clothes. His shirt was so full of holes that it scarcely covered his back.

"What are you spinning?" he asked.

The Princess had not known, until that moment, what she was spinning, but now she understood at once.

"I am spinning to make you a new shirt," she said.

"Oh, thank you!" said the little boy as he smiled down at her. The Princess looked at him, wondering. She noticed that his eyes looked very like those of her fairy-godmother.

Then she thought of something else.

"In the little house you will find a treasure," her fairy-godmother had said.

She looked all about. There was no gold, or anything that she had thought before was a treasure there. Then she listened to her heart that was singing, too, now. That was it. Her fairy-godmother had given her, in her little house, the treasure of a happy heart.

THE OLD HOUSE

Up there in the street was an old, old house.

All the other houses in the street were new, with large window panes and smooth walls, but the old house had queer faces cut out of the beams over the windows, and under the eaves was a dragon's head for a rain-water spout. The front steps were as broad as those to a palace, and as high, it seemed, as to a church tower.

"How long is that old place to stand and spoil our street?" said the families who lived in the new houses.

But at the window opposite the old house there sat a little boy with rosy cheeks and bright eyes. He certainly liked the old house best, in sunshine or when the moon shone on it. He knew who lived there, an old man who wore a coat with large brass buttons and a wig which one could see was really a wig. Every morning there came an ancient servant to put his rooms in order and to do his errands. Now and then the old man came to the window and looked out, and the little boy nodded to him, and the old man nodded back as if he were pleased. The little boy heard his father and mother say,

"The old man opposite is rich, but he is so very, very lonely."

The Sunday following the little boy took something, and wrapped it up in a piece of paper. He went downstairs and stood in the doorway, and when the errand man came past, he said to him,

"I say, sir, will you give this to the old man over the way for me? I have two toy soldiers. This is one of them and he shall have it, for I hear that he is lonely."

The errand man looked pleased, nodded, and took the toy soldier over to the old house. Afterwards there came a message; it was to ask if the little boy himself would not come over and pay a visit. So he got permission of his mother, and went over to the old house.

It seemed as if the brass balls on the iron fence shone brighter than ever because he had come. There were steps in the garden that went down and then up again, and the porch, even, was overgrown with green stuff as if it were part of the garden. The walls of the hall were hung with musty leather, printed with gold flowers, and there were chairs with high backs that creaked as if they had the gout.

And at last the little boy came into the room where the old man sat.

"I thank you for the toy soldier, my little friend," said the old man, "and I thank you because you came over to see me."

The pendulum of the great clock went to and fro, and the hands turned, and everything in the room became still older, but the little boy went up to the old man and took his hand.

"They said at home," said the little boy, "that you were very lonely."

Then the old man took a book with pictures in it down from a shelf, and he went into the other room to the pantry. It was really delightful in the old house!

But the toy soldier, who sat on a cabinet, suddenly spoke.

"I can't bear it any longer," he said. "The days are so dull and the evenings are still duller. Here it is not at all like your home, where your father and mother talk so pleasantly, and you and the other children make such a delightful noise."

"Oh, you mustn't mind that," said the little boy. "This house is full of old thoughts that come and visit and bring much company with them."

"I see nothing of them, and I don't know them because I am new," said the toy soldier. "I cannot bear it!"

"But you must!" said the little boy.

Then in came the old man with the most pleased and happy face, and bringing such delicious sweets, apples, and nuts. So the little boy thought no more about the toy soldier.

He went home, happy. Weeks and days passed, and he nodded over to the old house, and the old man nodded back. Then the little boy went over again.

The old man went to find a treasure box that he had with secret drawers, and the toy soldier took this opportunity of speaking once more to the little boy.

"Do you still sing on Sundays?" he asked. "When the curtains are up I can see you all over there at home distinctly. Tell me about my brother. Does he still live? Yes, he is happy then. Oh, I cannot bear it here any longer."

"You are given away as a present," the little boy said. "You will have to stay. Can't you try and make the best of it?"

The old man came in now with the box. Secret springs released the drawers and in these were cards, large and gilded, such as one never sees now. Then he opened the piano. It had landscapes painted on the inside of the lid. It was very hoarse but the old man could play on it and he sang a song too.

"I will go to the wars! I will go to the wars!" shouted the toy soldier as loudly as he could, and he threw himself off the cabinet right down on the floor.

Where was he? The old man looked, and the little boy looked, but the soldier was away and he stayed away.

"I shall find him!" said the old man, but he never did. The floor was too open. The toy soldier had fallen through a crack, and there he lay.

The little boy went home, and that week passed, and several weeks too. The windows were frosted; the little boy had to breathe on them to get a peep over at the old house; and snow covered the carved heads over the windows. The old house looked very cold, but now there was no one at home in it. And when the spring came they pulled the house down.

After a while a fine house was built in its place with large windows and smooth white walls. Before it, where part of the old house had stood, a garden was laid out and there were grape vines running along the walks. Birds built their nests in the vines and chattered away to each other, but not about the old house, for they could not remember it, so many years had passed. So many years had gone by that the little boy had grown up to a whole man. And he had just been married and had brought his wife to live in the house here, where the garden was. She had brought a wild flower with her that she found very pretty and he stood by her as she planted it in the garden and pressed the earth around it with her fingers.

Oh, what was that? She had pricked her finger. There sat something pointed, sticking straight out of the soft mould.

It was—yes, guess—it was the toy soldier who had tumbled and turned about among the timber and the rubbish, and had lain for many years in the ground.

The young wife wiped the dirt off the soldier, first with a green leaf, and then with her fine handkerchief. It was just as if the toy soldier had awakened from a dream. Then the young man told his wife about the old house and the old man and the toy soldier that he had sent over because the old man had been so lonely.

"Very, very lonely!" said the toy soldier, "but it is delightful not to be forgotten!"

THE LITTLE BOY WHO WANTED A CASTLE

There was once a boy who thought a great deal about castles. He had a very beautiful picture book with coloured pictures of castles that showed how large and different and fine they were, and, presently, after thinking a long time about it, the boy decided that a castle was where he would like, most of all, to live.

So very early one morning, when it was a sunny day and pleasant enough for any sort of an adventure, the boy made up his mind that he would go out for a little journey and try to find himself a castle.

He told his mother about it, for he always told her everything, and she smiled down into his face as she buttoned his coat.

"Are you sure that you can find a castle?" she asked.

"Oh, yes indeed, very sure," the boy answered. "And if I can't I'll ask some one on the road and he'll be able to tell me."

"Well, don't go so far away from home as to be late for supper," said his mother, kissing him good-bye. And the boy said good-bye to his mother and started off, but he made up his mind that probably he wouldn't be home that night because he would be having his supper in his castle.

The road was wide, and long, and winding, and the boy went down it for a long way. He saw no great golden castle, only pleasant little white houses with gardens, and people passing by with loads of vegetables and fruit and flowers going to the town. At last he came to a sharp turn in the road, and he saw an old man standing there with his dog.

"Please, sir," asked the boy, "I am taking a journey to find a castle. Can you tell me how to find one?"

The old man looked surprised. "I've heard about castles around here," he said, "but I don't know as you'll find one in a day. You'll know one, though, by the gold on the roof," he explained.

So the boy went on farther still, and he came to another turn in the road. A girl with her flock of geese stood there, and the boy spoke to her. "I am taking a journey to a castle," he said. "Can you tell me how to find one?"

The girl laughed. "You'll know it by the garden," she said. "All castles have very pretty gardens."

So the boy went farther still, and where the road curved he met an old granny walking toward him with her knitting in her hand.

"Please, granny," said the boy. "I am taking a journey to find a castle. Can you direct me to one?"

The granny looked down through her spectacles at the boy. "Perhaps you will come to a castle beyond the last turn in the road," she said, pointing behind her. "They say there are castles hidden hereabouts. You'll know it by the fine feasts they give every day at sundown, and the king and queen will be waiting at the door to welcome you."

"How shall I know the king and queen? Do they always wear crowns?" asked the little boy.

"Not always," said the granny, "but you can tell a true king and queen because they are so good and wise and kind."

So the boy thanked the granny and went on, but it was growing late in the day and he was tired. The bend in the road seemed a very long way off and he had to sit down several times before he reached it. His feet ached and his back was tired when he came to it, but when he turned and came out on the other side, he saw something wonderful.

Just a little way ahead lay the castle.

He could be quite sure that it was a castle because the roof shone with gold in the setting sun and in front lay a pretty garden of flowers of all kinds; pink roses, and tall white lilies, and purple violets. In the doorway stood two people waiting; they must be the king and queen, thought the little boy. As he ran and came nearer, he could smell the feast—a savoury meat pie, and freshly baked cake, and sweet fruits.

The boy ran faster and came to the gate and went up the walk. At the doorway he stopped. Why, it was his own house that he had come back to by way of the turns in the road. This was his own pretty garden that he saw, and his own fine supper that he smelled. His own dear father and mother waited in the door, with their arms outstretched to greet him.

"You are the king and queen," shouted the boy, "always good and kind!"

"And this is our castle," laughed his mother. "Come in, my little Prince. The feast is waiting for you."

THE CHILDREN

THE PLAYMATES

There was once a Prince and he was very lonely, because he had no sisters or brothers in the palace with whom to play. And one day his father and mother, the King and Queen, decided that they would send to some neighboring Kingdoms to borrow a little Princess, who should come and live at the palace, and be the sister and the playmate of the Prince.

So they sent for one of the Court Messengers, and then they called the Prince to tell him that he was going to have a little Princess to be his playmate.

They talked the matter over with the Court Wise-Man that the Messenger might understand just what sort of little Princess he should bring, and make no mistake about it.

"She must be sweet tempered," said the King.

"And I should like her to have blue eyes and yellow hair and curls," said the Queen.

"And if I may be so bold as to make a suggestion," said the Court Wise-Man, "she should be rich, for she and the Prince will need a great many new toys."

They never thought to ask the Prince what his choice of a little Princess would be. But the Prince did not wait to be asked.

"I want only a little Princess who can make molasses pop-corn balls," he said.

The King and the Queen and the Court Wise-Man were aghast at this. They knew that the Prince was very fond of molasses pop-corn balls, but the palace Cook always made him some every Saturday morning, enough to last a whole week. But the Prince went on, and explained.

"The Princess who comes to play with me must be able to do what I want her to, and I want her to make my pop-corn balls fresh every day. Don't bring any Princess who can't," he said.

So they all knew that the matter was decided, for the Prince had a very strong mind of his own. The Court Messenger started out to find a little Princess who was sweet tempered, and had blue eyes, and yellow hair that curled, and was rich, and knew how to make molasses pop-corn balls.

He thought that he would find the right Princess overnight, but it came to be weeks and weeks and she was still as far away as ever. The Princesses who were sweet tempered were apt to have brown hair and hazel eyes, and if there was a sweet tempered one with blue eyes and yellow hair that curled she belonged in a Kingdom where there was very little money. And none of the Princesses had even so much as heard of molasses pop-corn balls. The Court Messenger grew so worried that he could neither eat nor sleep, but one day as he wandered about in foreign places he smelled something like molasses boiling. He followed the odor and he came to a rich appearing palace. In he went, without waiting to knock, and beside the kitchen fireplace he discovered a Princess with blue eyes and yellow hair that curled. She was stirring molasses in a kettle with one hand, and shaking a corn popper with the other.

"What are you making?" begged the Messenger in great excitement.

"Molasses pop-corn balls," said the little Princess.

"Are you sweet tempered?" asked the Messenger.

"I never cry, or scold," said the little Princess.

"Then come with me and be the Prince's playmate," said the Messenger. "We must have a Princess who will make him pop-corn balls every day."

The little Princess looked up in surprise. "Can the Prince play to me on a jews-harp?" she asked.

"I do not think his Highness can," said the Messenger.

"Then I can't go with you," said the little Princess. "I will go only to a Prince who can play on a jews-harp."

"I won't learn to play on a jews-harp," said the little Prince when they told him about it.

So he was without a sister and a playmate, and every day he grew more lonely and more unhappy. But he thought a great deal and at last he said:

"I should like to have that little Princess very much. Will you ask her if she will come if she does not have to make molasses pop-corn balls?"

Now, all this time, the Princess had been thinking too. When the Court Messenger gave her the Prince's message, she smiled and said she would come. "The Prince need not play to me on a jews-harp if he does not want to," she said.

So they packed her clothes in ten trunks, and she rode in a gold chariot to the palace of the Prince. The doors were opened wide to greet her, and through them came the sound of the merriest music. The Princess clasped her hands in happiness.

"Who is playing the jews-harp?" she asked. "I am so fond of one."

Just then the Prince came in. It had been he who was playing. He had learned how for her pleasure.

"What are you carrying in that basket?" he asked of the little Princess.

"Some molasses pop-corn balls that I made for you," she said. "And I will make you some to-morrow, dear Prince."

THE STAR-CHILD

Once upon a time a poor Woodcutter was making his way through a pine forest. It was winter, and a night of bitter weather. So cold was it that even the animals and the birds did not know what to make of it. The little Squirrels who lived inside the tall fir tree kept rubbing each other's noses to keep warm, and the Rabbits curled themselves up in their holes and did not even look out of doors.

And as the Woodcutter pressed on toward home, bewailing his lot, there fell from heaven a very bright and beautiful star. It slipped down the side of the sky, passing by the other stars, and it seemed to sink behind a clump of willow trees no more than a stone's throw away.

"Why, there is a crock of gold for whoever finds it," he said, and he hastened toward it. Stooping down, he placed his hands upon a thing of gold lying on the white snow. It was a cloak of golden tissue, curiously wrought with stars, and wrapped in many folds. There was no gold in it, but only a little child who was asleep.

Very tenderly the Woodcutter took up the child and wrapped the cloak around it to shield it from the harsh cold, and he made his way down the hill to the village.

"I have found something in the forest," he said to his wife when he reached the poor house where they lived.

"What is it?" she cried. "The house is bare and we have need of many things." So he drew the cloak back and showed her the sleeping child.

"It is a Star-Child," he said, and told her of the strange manner of finding it.

"But our children lack bread; can we feed another?" she asked.

"God careth for the sparrows even," he answered.

So after a time she turned round and looked at him, and her eyes were full of tears. And he came in swiftly, and placed the child in her arms, and she kissed it, and laid it in a little bed where the youngest of their own children was lying. And on the morrow the Woodcutter took the curious cloak of gold and placed it in a great chest, and a chain of amber that was round the child's neck his wife took and set in the chest also.

So the Star-Child was brought up with the children of the Woodcutter, and sat at the same board with them, and was their playmate. And every year he became more beautiful to look at, so that all those who dwelt in the village were filled with wonder. While they were swarthy and black-haired, he was white and delicate as ivory, and his curls were like the rings of the daffodil. His lips, also, were like the petals of a red flower, and his eyes were like violets, and his body like a narcissus of a field where the mower comes not.

Yet, the Star-Child's beauty worked him harm, for he grew proud and cruel and selfish. He despised the other children of the village because they were of mean parentage, and he made himself master of them and called them his servants. He had no pity for the poor, or for those who were blind, or lame; but would cast stones at them.

Now there passed one day through the village a poor beggar-woman. Her garments were torn and ragged, and her feet were bleeding from the rough road on which she had travelled, and she was in very evil plight. And being weary, she sat her down under a chestnut-tree to rest.

But when the Star-Child saw her, he said to his companions, "See! There sits a beggar-woman under that fair and green-leaved tree. Come, let us drive her hence, for she is ugly and ill-favoured."

So he came near and threw stones at her, and mocked her, and, she looked at him with terror in her eyes, nor did she move her gaze from him.

"Whose child is this?" she asked. Then the Woodcutter, who was passing by, told of finding the Star-Child, of the chain of amber around his neck and the cloak wrought with stars. And, hearing, the beggar-woman cried with joy.

"He is my little son," she said, "whom I lost through enchantment in the forest. I have searched for him through all the world."

The Woodcutter called the Star-Child, and said to him,

"Here is thy mother, waiting for thee."

But the Star-Child laughed scornfully.

"I am no son of thine," he said. "I am a Star-Child, and thou art a beggar, and ugly, and in rags. Get thee hence that I may see thee no more."

"Oh, my little son," cried the beggar-woman. "Will you not kiss me before I go? I have suffered much to find thee."

"No," said the Star-Child. "I would rather kiss an adder or a toad than thee."

So the woman went away into the forest, weeping bitterly, and the Star-Child was glad and ran back to his playmates. But when they saw him coming they ran away from him in fear. He went to the well and looked in.

Lo, his face was as the face of a toad and his body was scaled like an adder. He flung himself down on the grass, and wept.

"I denied my mother," he said. "This has come upon me because of my sin. I will seek her through all the world, nor rest until I have found her."

So he ran away into the forest and called out to his mother to come to him, but there was no answer. All day long he called to her, and when the sun set he lay down to sleep on a bed of leaves, and the birds and the animals fled from him, for they remembered his cruelty, and he was alone save for the toad that watched him, and the slow adder that crawled past.

And in the morning he rose up and plucked some bitter berries from the trees and ate them, and took his way through the great wood, weeping sorely. And of everything that he met he made inquiry if perchance they had seen his mother.

He said to the Mole, "Thou canst go beneath the earth. Tell me, is my mother there?"

And the Mole answered, "Thou hast blinded mine eyes. How should I know?"

He said to the Linnet, "Thou canst fly over the tops of the tall trees and canst see the whole world. Tell me, canst thou see my mother?"

And the Linnet answered, "Thou hast clipt my wings for thy pleasure. How should I fly?"

And to the little Squirrel who lived in the fir tree, and was lonely, he said, "Where is my mother?"

And the Squirrel answered, "Thou hast slain mine. Dost thou seek to slay thine also?"

And the Star-Child wept and bowed his head and prayed forgiveness of God's things, and went on through the forest, seeking for the beggar-woman.

When he passed through the villages the children mocked him and threw stones at him. He had no place to rest his head, and none had pity on him. For the space of three years he wandered over the world, and often seemed to see his mother in the road in front of him, and would call to her, and run after her until the sharp flints made his feet bleed. But overtake her he could not, and there was neither love nor charity for him. It was such a world as he had made for himself in the days of his pride.

It happened that in his wanderings he was taken and sold as a slave, and his master, who was a wicked magician, demanded that he go out in search of a piece of pure white gold.

"See that thou bringest it," said the magician, "or it will go hard with thee."

So the Star-Child went in search of the piece of white gold but he could not find it, although he sought for it from morn to noon, and from noon to sunset. Then he set his face toward home, weeping bitterly, for he knew that the magician would beat him with an hundred stripes. But suddenly he heard, from a thicket a cry, and, forgetting his own sorrow, he ran to the place. He saw a little Hare caught in a trap.

The Star-Child had pity on it and released it and the Hare said to him, "What shall I give thee in return for my freedom?"

And the Star-Child said to it, "I am seeking for a piece of white gold nor can I, anywhere, find it; and if I bring it not to my master he will beat me."

"Come with me," said the Hare. "I know where it is hidden, and for what purpose."

So the Star-Child went with the Hare, and in the cleft of a great oak tree he saw the white gold that he was seeking. He took it and ran swiftly toward the city.

Now at the gate of the city there was seated one who was a leper. When he saw the Star-Child he called to him and said, "Give me a piece of money or I must die of hunger. They have turned me out of the city and there is no one who has pity on me."

"Alas," cried the Star-Child. "I have but one piece of money, and if I bring it not to my master he will beat me, for I am his slave."

"Give me the piece of money or I must die," cried the leper and the Star-Child had pity on him and gave him the piece of gold. Yet his heart was heavy, for he knew what evil fate awaited him.

But, lo, as he passed through the gates of the city, the guards bowed to him and the high officers of the city ran forth to meet him and cried, "Thou art our lord for whom we have been waiting, and the son of our king."

And the Star-Child wondered.

"I am no king's son, but the child of a beggar-woman and evil to look at," he said. Then he saw his image in one of the burnished shields of the guards.

Lo, his face was again beautiful, and all his comeliness had come back to him again.

But he said to them, "I am not worthy, for I have denied my mother, nor may I rest until I have found her. Let me go, for I must wander again through the world." As he spoke he looked toward the road and there he saw the beggar-woman who was his mother and at her side stood the leper who had sat beside the gate.

Then a cry of joy broke from the Star-Child's lips and he ran over, and kneeled down, and kissed the wounds in his mother's feet. And the beggar-woman put her hand on his head and said to him, "Rise"; and the leper put his hand upon the Star-Child also, and said to him, "Rise."

And he rose up from their feet and looked at them; and they were a King and a Queen.

And the Queen said to him, "This is thy father whom thou hast fed."

And the King said, "This is thy mother whose feet thou hast washed with thy tears."

And they clothed the Star-Child in fair raiment and set a crown upon his head and a sceptre in his hand and he was the ruler of the city. He was wise and merciful to all, and to the Woodcutter and his family he sent many rich gifts. He would not suffer any one to be cruel to bird or beast, but taught love and loving kindness; and to the poor he gave bread, and to the naked raiment; and there was peace and plenty in the land.

OLE LUK-OIE

In the whole world there is nobody who knows so many stories as Ole Luk-Oie. He really can tell stories.

It is in the evening, when the children are sitting nicely at table, or upon their stools, that Ole Luk-Oie comes. Softly he creeps up the stairs, for he walks in socks; opens the door very gently, and squirts sweet milk in the children's eyes—whisk! just a tiny drop, but quite enough to prevent them from keeping their eyes open; and so they cannot see him.

Then he steals just behind them, and blows softly at the back of their necks, so that their heads become heavy. But of course it does not hurt them, for Ole Luk-Oie is fond of the children, and only wants them to be quiet. They are most quiet when they are in bed; and they have to be quiet indeed when Ole Luk-Oie tells them his stories.

When the children are nearly asleep, Ole Luk-Oie seats himself upon the bed. He is neatly dressed; his coat is of silk, but it is impossible to say of what color, for it shines green, red, and blue, according to which side he turns. Under each arm he carries an umbrella. One is lined with pictures, and this he spreads over the good children, so that they dream the most beautiful stories the whole night through; but on the other umbrella there are no pictures, and this he holds over the naughty children, so that they sleep heavily, and when they awake in the morning they have not dreamed at all.

We shall now hear how Ole Luk-Oie came to a little boy named Hjalmar, and what he told him.

Over the chest of drawers in Hjalmar's room hung a large picture in a gilt frame. It was a landscape. One could see tall trees, and flowers in the grass. There was a great lake, and a river that flowed round the forest, past castles, and out and out into the sea.

Ole Luk-Oie touched the painting with his magic squirt, and the birds in it began to sing, the branches of the trees moved, and the clouds floated along. Then Ole Luk-Oie lifted little Hjalmar up to the frame, and Hjalmar put his feet into the picture, right into the high grass; and there he stood, with the sun shining upon him. He ran to the water and seated himself in a little boat that lay there; it was painted red and white, and the sails gleamed with silver. Six swans, wearing golden circlets around their necks and twinkling blue stars on their heads, drew the boat.

Gorgeous fishes, with scales of silver and gold, swam after the boat, sometimes springing high into the air and falling back with a splash into the water. They wanted all to follow Hjalmar, and each one had a story to tell.

It was really a beautiful voyage. At one time the forests were thick and dark, at another they looked like a glorious garden full of sunlight and flowers. There were great palaces of glass and marble; on the balconies stood Princesses, and they were all little girls whom Hjalmar knew well — he had played with them before. Each one stretched forth her hand, and held out the prettiest sugar pig that a cake-woman could sell. Hjalmar took hold of one end of the sugar pig as he passed by, but the Princess also held fast, so that each of them got a piece — she the smaller part, and Hjalmar the larger.

Before each palace stood little Princes as sentries. They presented arms with golden swords, and then it rained raisins and tin soldiers; they were real Princes. At one moment Hjalmar was sailing through forests, at another through great halls, or straight through the middle of a town.

Ole Luk-Oie had taken Hjalmar for a wonderful journey that night.

And another night Ole Luk-Oie said to Hjalmar, "Don't be afraid. I will show you a little mouse," and he held out his hand with the pretty little creature. "It has come to invite you to a wedding. Two little Mice are going to be married to-night. They live under the floor of your mother's pantry; it is said to be such a nice place to live in."

"But how can I get through the mouse hole in the floor?" asked Hjalmar.

"I will see to that," said Ole Luk-Oie. And with his magic squirt he touched Hjalmar, who at once began to grow smaller and smaller, until at last he was scarcely as big as a finger.

"Now you can borrow the tin soldier's uniform. I think it will fit you," said Ole Luk-Oie.

And in a moment Hjalmar was dressed like the smartest of tin soldiers.

"Will you be so kind as to take a seat in your Mamma's thimble?" said the mouse; "I shall then have the honour of drawing you."

"Oh, dear! are you going to take this trouble yourself, little miss?" said Hjalmar.

Then they drove to the mouse's wedding. They passed first through a long passage beneath the floor, which was only just high enough to drive through in a thimble; and the whole passage was lit up with phosphorescent wood.

"Doesn't it smell nice here?" said the mouse, who was drawing the thimble. "The whole passage has been greased with bacon fat; it could not be more exquisite."

Then they came into the bridal hall. On the right hand stood all the little lady mice; and they whispered and giggled as if they were making fun of one another; on the left stood all the gentlemen mice, stroking their whiskers with their forepaws; and in the center of the hall you could see the bride and bridegroom, standing in a hollow cheese.

More and more guests arrived, until the mice were nearly treading one another to death. The bridal pair had stationed themselves just in the doorway, so that one could neither come in nor go out. Like the passage, the floor had been greased with bacon fat, and that was the whole of the feast; but for dessert they produced a pea on which a mouse belonging to the family had bitten the name of the bridal pair — that is to say, the first letter of the name. It was something extraordinary.

All the mice said it was a beautiful wedding, and that the entertainment had been very enjoyable.

So Hjalmar drove home again. He had been in very distinguished society; but he had been obliged to shrink together to make himself small, and to put on the tin soldier's uniform.

"Am I to hear any more stories now?" asked little Hjalmar, as soon as Ole Luk-Oie had put him to bed Saturday night.

"We have no time for that this evening," said Ole Luk-Oie; and he spread his finest umbrella over the child. "Now look at these Chinamen."

And the whole umbrella looked like a great china bowl, with blue trees and painted bridges, upon which stood little Chinamen, nodding their heads.

"We must have the whole world nicely cleaned up for to-morrow morning," said Ole Luk-Oie, "for it is a holiday—it is Sunday. I must go to the church steeple to see that the little church goblins are polishing the bells, so that they may sound sweetly. I must go out into the fields, and see that the winds are blowing the dust from the grass and leaves; and—this is the greatest work of all—I must bring down all the stars to polish them. I have to number each one of them before I take them in my apron, and the holes in which they are up there must be numbered as well, so that they may be put back in their right places, or they would not stick firmly, and then we should have too many shooting-stars, for they would be dropping down one after the other!"

"Do you know, Mr. Luk-Oie," said an old portrait, which hung on the wall in the room where Hjalmar slept, "that I am Hjalmar's great-grandfather? I am much obliged to you for telling the boy stories; but you must not confuse ideas. The stars cannot be taken down and polished. They are spheres, just like our earth, and that is just the best thing about them."

"I thank you, old grandfather," said Ole Luk-Oie, "I thank you! You are the head of the family, the ancestral head: but I am older than you! I am an old heathen; the Romans and Greeks called me the Dream God. I have been in the noblest houses, and am admitted there still. I know how to act with great people and with small. Now you can tell your story!"

Ole Luk-Oie took his umbrella, and went away.

And Hjalmar awoke.

THE FAMILY

WHAT FATHER DOES IS ALWAYS RIGHT

I have no doubt that you have been out in the country, and have seen a real old farm-house, with a thatched roof, and moss, and plants growing wild upon it. There is a stork's nest on the ridge, for one cannot very well do without the stork; the walls are sloping, the windows low, and the baking-oven projects from the wall like a fat little body. The elder-tree hangs over the fence, and there is a little pool of water, with a duck and her ducklings, beneath some old willow-trees. There is, also, a dog that barks at everybody who passes by.

Just such an old farm-house stood out in the country, and there lived an old couple, a peasant and his wife. Little though they had, there was one thing they could not do without, and that was the horse, that found a living by grazing on the roadside.

Father rode on it to town, and the neighbours borrowed it; but the old couple thought it might perhaps be better to sell the horse or exchange it for something more useful.

"You will know best, father, what this something should be," said the wife. "To-day is market-day in town; ride down there and sell the horse or make a good exchange. What you do is always right—so ride to the market."

So she wrapped his muffler around him, for she could do this better than he, and tied it in a double knot, so that it looked very smart; then she brushed his hat with the palm of her hand, and gave him a hearty kiss. He rode away on the horse that was about to be sold or exchanged. Yes; father knew what he was about!

A man came along, leading a cow—as pretty a cow as one could wish to see.

"She must give good milk, I am sure," thought the peasant; "it would be a very good exchange to get her for the horse. Hello there, you, with the cow!" he cried, "let us have a little chat. Of course, a horse costs more than a cow, but I don't mind that; I happen to have more use for the cow. Shall we make an exchange?"

"All right," said the man with the cow, and so they exchanged.

Now that the bargain was made, the peasant might have returned home, for he had finished his business; but, as he had made up his mind to go to market, he thought he might as well do so, if only to see what was going on. So off he walked with his cow.

He walked quickly, and the cow walked quickly, and so they soon overtook a man who was leading a sheep. It was a fine sheep, in good condition, and with plenty of wool.

"Now, that is just the thing I should like to have," thought the peasant. "There is plenty of grass for it by the roadside, and in the winter we could take it into the house with us. As a matter of fact, it would be more suitable for us to keep than a cow. Shall we exchange?" he asked.

The man with the sheep was quite willing; so the exchange was made.

The peasant went along the road with his sheep, and at the stile he met a man with a big goose under his arm.

"That is a heavy bird you have there," said the peasant, "with plenty of feather and fat. It would look capital tied with a piece of string by the pond. It would be something for the wife to save the potato peelings for. She has so often said: 'If we only had a goose!' and now she can get one, and we shall have it. Shall we exchange? I will give you the sheep for the goose, and thank you into the bargain," said the peasant. The other man was quite willing; and so they exchanged, and the peasant got the goose.

He was now close to the town. The crowd on the road became greater, and there was a crush and a rush of men and cattle. They were walking on the road and by the roadside, and at the turn-pike-gate they walked even in the toll-man's potato-field, where a hen was strutting about with a string tied to her leg, in order that she should not go astray in the crowd and so get lost. It was a nice fat hen; it winked with one eye, and looked very artful. "Cluck! cluck!" it said; what it thought, when saying it, I do not know; but the peasant thought, as he saw the hen,

"Now, that is the nicest hen I have ever seen. She is finer than our parson's hen. I should like to have her. A hen can always pick up something; she can almost keep herself. I think it would be a good exchange if I got her for the goose. Shall we exchange?" he said.

"Exchange!" said the other; "that wouldn't be so bad." So they exchanged; the toll-man got the goose, and the peasant got the hen.

He had done a good deal of business on his way to town; it was very hot, and he was very tired; he would be all the better for a piece of bread, and now he was at the inn.

He was going in, and the innkeeper was going out, so they met in the doorway.

The innkeeper carried a big sack of something.

"What have you there?" said the peasant.

"Apples!" answered the man; "a whole sackful for the pigs."

"Oh, that is a rare lot; I should like mother to see them. Last year we had only one single apple on the old tree by the peat-house; this apple we kept on the top of the cupboard until it cracked. 'Well, it is always property,' said mother; but here she could see any quantity of property; yes, I should like to show them to her."

"Well, what will you give for them?" asked the man.

"What will I give? I'll give my hen in exchange," he said, and so he gave his hen in exchange, got the apples, and went into the inn.

Many strangers were present in the room, and they soon heard the whole story—how the horse was exchanged for the cow, and so on, down to the apples.

"Well, your good wife will give it to you when you get home," said one of them.

"Not at all," said the peasant; "she will give me a kiss, instead of scolding me, and she will say: 'What father does is always right.'"

"Shall we wager," said the stranger, "a barrel of gold coins—a hundred pounds to a hundredweight?"

"It is quite enough to make it a bushelful," said the peasant; "I can only set the bushel of apples against it; but I will throw myself and the wife into the bargain, and that, I should say, is good measure!"

"Done!" he said; and so the wager was made.

The innkeeper's carriage came up, and the stranger got in, the peasant got in, and the apples got in, and away they all went to the peasant's house.

"Good evening, mother!"

"Good evening, father!"

"I have made the exchange."

"Well, you understand what you are about," said the woman, and she was so glad to see him, she forgot all about the sack and the stranger.

"I have exchanged the horse for a cow."

"Oh, how nice to get milk!" said the wife; "now we can have butter and cheese on the table; that was indeed a capital exchange!"

"Yes, but I exchanged the cow for a sheep."

"Well, that is perhaps better," said the wife; "you always think of everything. We have just enough pasture for a sheep; ewe's milk, and cheese, and woolen socks, and a woolen jacket—the cow cannot give these. How you do think of everything, to be sure!"

"But the sheep I exchanged for a goose."

"Are we really going to have roast goose for Christmas this year, father dear? You are always thinking of something to please me. This is a capital idea of yours; the goose can be tied to a string, and we will fatten her for Christmas!"

"But I exchanged the goose for a hen," said the old man.

"A hen! oh, that was a good bargain!" said the woman. "A hen lays eggs, and hatches them, and so we can get chickens—a whole poultry-yard—and that's the very thing I have always wished for."

"Yes; but the hen I exchanged for a sack of apples!"

"Now, I must really kiss you!" said the woman.

"Thank you, thank you, my dear man! Now I'll tell you something; when you were gone, I thought I would make a nice meal for you—pancakes with onions. The eggs I had, but I had no onions, so I went over to the school-master's—they have onions, I know, but the wife is mean, poor thing. I asked her to lend me some. 'Lend!' she said; 'there is nothing that grows in our garden that I could lend you—not even an apple.' But now I can lend her ten, or a whole sackful—that is really nice, father."

"Well, that is capital!" exclaimed the stranger, "always going downhill, and yet always cheerful; it is worth the money." So he paid a hundredweight of gold to the peasant.

Now, that is my story. I heard it when I was little, and now you have heard it too, and know that what father does is always right.

THE ELDER TREE MOTHER

There was once a little boy who had caught cold; he had gone out and got wet feet. No one could imagine how it had happened, for it was quite dry weather. His mother undressed him, put him to bed, and had the tea-urn brought in to make him a good cup of elder tea, for that warms well.

"Now you are to drink your tea," said the mother, "and then perhaps you will hear a story."

The little boy drank the elder tea and then looked at the tea-pot. The lid raised itself and the elder flowers came forth from it, white and fresh. They shot forth long branches even out of the spout; they spread about in all directions and became larger and larger. There was the most glorious elder bush, in fact quite a tree. It stretched to the bed and thrust the curtains aside; how fragrant it was and how it bloomed! And in the midst of the tree sat an old, pleasant looking woman in a strange dress. It was quite green like the leaves of the elder tree, and bordered with great white elder blossoms. One could not tell whether this border was of stuff, or of living green and real flowers.

"Who are you?" the little boy asked.

"They used to call me a Dryad," said the woman, "but I have a better name than that. I am the Elder Tree Mother."

Then she took the little boy out of bed, and laid him upon her bosom. The blossoming elder branches wound round them so they sat as it were in the thickest arbor, and this arbor flew away with them through the air. It was very beautiful. Elder Mother all at once became a pretty young girl; at her throat she had a real elder flower, and on her head a wreath of elder blossoms. Her eyes were large and blue. She and the boy were of the same age and felt the same joys.

Hand in hand they went out of the arbor, and now they stood in the beauteous flower garden of home. The father's staff was tied up near the fresh grass plot, and for the little boy there was life in the staff. The polished head turned into a noble, neighing horse's head with a flowing mane, and four slender legs shot forth. They seated themselves upon it and began to ride miles away. And the little girl who, as we know, was no one else but Elder Mother, cried out,

"Now we're in the country. Do you see the farm-house with the great baking oven standing out of the wall? The elder tree spreads its branches over it, and the cock walks about, scratching for his hens. Look how he struts!

"Now we are at the forge where the fire burns and the hammers send bright sparks flying far around. But away, away!"

Everything, and more than the little girl mentioned as she sat on the stick behind him, flew past them. He will never forget, and throughout their whole journey the elder tree smelled so fresh, so fragrant. He noticed the roses and the fresh beech trees, but the elder tree smelled stronger than all for its flowers hung round the little girl and he often leaned against them as they flew onward.

"Here it is beautiful in spring!" said the little girl.

And they stood in the green beech wood where the thyme lay in fragrance beneath their feet and pink anemones looked pretty against the green.

"Here it is beautiful in summer!" said she.

And they passed by old castles where swans swam about and they looked down the shady avenues. In the fields the corn waved like a sea. In the ditches yellow and red flowers were growing, and in the hedges wild hops. In the evening the moon rose, round and large, and the haystacks in the meadows smelled sweet.

"Here it is beautiful in autumn!" said the little girl.

And the sky seemed twice as lofty and twice as blue as before and the forests were decked in the most gorgeous tints of red, yellow, and green. Whole flocks of wild ducks flew screaming overhead. The sea was dark blue and covered with ships with white sails; and in the barns sat old women, girls, and children picking hops into a large tub. The young people sang songs and the older ones told tales of goblins. It could hardly be finer anywhere.

"Here it is beautiful in winter!" said the little girl.

All the trees were covered with hoar frost so that they looked like white trees of coral. The snow creaked beneath one's boots as if every one had new boots on, and one shooting star after another fell from the sky. In the houses Christmas trees were lighted, and there were presents and there was happiness. In the country people's farm-houses the violin sounded, and there were merry games for apples. Even the poorest child said, "It is beautiful in winter!"

So the little girl showed the boy everything, and suddenly the boy grew up and was to go out into the wide world, far away to the hot countries where the coffee grows. When they were to part the little girl took an elder blossom from her wreath and gave it to him to keep. He put it in a book, and the more he looked at the flower the fresher it became so that he seemed, as it were, to breathe the forest air of home. Then he plainly saw the little girl looking out with her clear blue eyes from between the petals of the flower and she whispered,

"Here it is beautiful in spring, summer, autumn, and winter!" and hundreds of pictures glided through his thoughts.

Many years went by. He seemed to be an old man and sat with his wife under the blossoming elder tree. The little maiden with the blue eyes and with the wreath of elder blossoms in her hair sat up in the tree, and nodded to both of them, and said, "To-day is our golden wedding day!" Then she took two flowers out of her hair and kissed them, and they gleamed, first, like silver, then like gold. When she laid them on the heads of the old people, each changed to a golden crown. There they both sat like a King and Queen, under a fragrant tree that looked quite like an elder bush; and he told his old wife the story of the Elder Tree Mother.

"Some call me Elder Tree Mother," said the little girl in the tree, "others the Dryad, but my real name is Remembrance. It is I who sit in the tree that grows on and on, and I can think back and tell stories. Let me see if you still have your flower?"

The old man opened his book; there lay the elder blossom as fresh as if it had only just been placed there; and Remembrance nodded, and the two old people with the golden crowns on their heads sat in the red evening sunlight, and they closed their eyes, and — the story was finished.

The little boy lay in his bed and did not know whether he had been dreaming or had heard a tale told. The tea-pot stood on the table, but no elder bush was growing out of it.

"How beautiful that was!" said the little boy. "Mother, I have been in the hot countries."

"Yes, I am sure of that!" replied the mother. "When one drinks two cups of hot elder tea one very often gets into the hot countries." And she covered him up well that he might not take cold. "You have slept well," she said.

"But where is the Elder Tree Mother?" asked the little lad.

"She's in the tea-pot," said his mother, "and there she may stay."

THE HAPPY FAMILY

The biggest leaf in the country is certainly the burdock leaf. Put one in front of your waist and it's just like an apron, and if you lay it upon your head it is almost as good as an umbrella, for it is remarkably large. Burdocks have another use. Snails feed on them.

Now there was an old estate where the burdocks grew and there was no stopping them. Here and there stood an apple or a plum tree; but for this nobody would have thought a garden had been there. Everywhere were burdocks, and among them lived two ancient white snails.

They did not know themselves how old they were, but they could very well remember that there had been a great many more of them; that they had descended from a large family. They led a very retired and happy life and, as they had no children, they had adopted a little common snail which they brought up as their own child. But the little thing would not grow, for he was only a common snail, although the mother declared that he was getting too large for his shell. And when the father noticed how small their child was, she told him to feel the little snail's shell, and he felt it, and said that she was right.

One day it rained very hard.

"Listen, how it's drumming on the burdock leaves, rum-dum-dum! rum-dum-dum!" said the Father Snail.

"That's what I call drops," said the Mother. "It's coming straight down the stalks. You'll see how wet the garden will be directly. I'm glad that we have our good houses and the little one has his own. There has been more done for us than for any other creature; one can see very plainly that we are the grand folks of the world! We have houses from our birth and the burdock forest has grown for us. I should like to know how far it extends and what lies beyond it."

"There's nothing," said the Father Snail, "that can be better than here at home. I have nothing at all to wish for. You must watch the little one. Has he not been creeping up the stalk these three days? My head quite aches when I look at him."

"Well, don't scold him," said the Mother Snail. "He crawls deliberately. We shall have much joy in him, and we old people have nothing else to live for.

But have you ever thought where we shall get a wife for him? Don't you think that farther in the wood there may be some more of our kind?"

"There may be black snails there, I think," said the Father Snail, — "black snails without houses! But they are too vulgar. And they're conceited at that. We can give the commission to the Ants, though; they run to and fro, as if they had business. They're sure to know of a wife for our young gentleman."

"I certainly know the most beautiful of brides," said one of the Ants, "but I fear she would not do, for she is the Queen."

"That does not matter," said the two old Snails. "Has she a house?"

"She has a castle!" replied the Ant, "the most beautiful ants' castle, with seven hundred passages."

"Thank you," said the Mother Snail, "our boy shall not go into an ant-hill. If you know of nothing better, we will give the commission to the white gnats. They fly far about in rain and sunshine, and they know the burdock wood, inside and outside."

"We have a wife for him," said the Gnats. "A hundred man-steps from here a little snail with a house is sitting on a gooseberry bush. She is quite alone, and old enough to marry. It's only a hundred man-steps from here."

"Yes, let her come to him," said the old people. "He has a whole burdock forest, and she has only a bush."

So they brought the little maiden Snail. Eight days passed before she arrived, but that was the rare circumstance by which one could see that she was of the right kind.

And then they had the wedding. Six Glow-Worms lighted as well as they could. With this exception it went very quietly, for the old Snails could not bear feasting and noise.

The Father Snail could not make a speech, he was so much moved; but he gave the young people the whole burdock forest for an inheritance. He said, what he and the Mother Snail had always said, that it was the best place in the world. And when the wedding was over, the old people crept into their houses and never came out again, for they slept.

The young Snail pair now ruled in the forest, and had a large family. The rain fell down upon the burdock leaves to play the drum for them. The sun shone to color the burdock forest for them; and they were happy, very happy. The whole family was uncommonly happy!

CLOTHING

THE WONDER SHOES

They looked like any other pair of boy's shoes, the same stout soles, strong lacings, shiny tips and uppers. But when the old shoemaker put them on Gustave, and laced them up, and saw that they exactly fitted, he said to Gustave:

"Wonder shoes, little man. They will be wonder shoes!"

The old shoemaker had lived a great many years. He had made shoes for Gustave's father, and when he said anything about heels or toes or leather it was quite sure to be true. But here was something very strange. Gustave's blue eyes looked and looked in surprise at his new shoes. They seemed not in the least different from those that he had just worn out, or those that he kept for Sunday. He glanced up at his mother, who was giving the shoemaker a shining silver dollar and a shining silver half dollar to pay for them. She did not say anything. She only smiled back into his eyes. Then Gustave spoke to the old shoemaker.

"Why are they wonder shoes?" he asked.

"Oh you will find out!" chuckled the old shoemaker as he patted Gustave's head. So Gustave and his mother went out of the old shoemaker's shop and up the street.

It was a windy, blustering day. The dry leaves were flying, and the weather cocks turned, creaking, around, and Gustave had to hold his head low for he was only a little boy and the wind nearly pushed him down. A bent old gentleman, walking with a cane, passed them. Puff, whisk, the wind took the old gentleman's hat and sent it racing ahead of him along the street.

But the wonder shoes were quicker than the wind. They carried Gustave like a flying breeze after the old gentleman's hat. He caught it, and picked it up and gave it back to the old gentleman, who was very grateful indeed, and gave Gustave a bright penny.

"A swift little boy!" exclaimed the old gentleman, but Gustave did not tell him about the wonder shoes. He had decided to keep that for a secret.

When Gustave and his mother reached home, his mother decided to make a loaf of white cake. But, alas; when she went to the pantry, she discovered that she had no butter.

"Run to the grocery shop, Gustave," she said, "and bring me back a pat of butter by the time that the fire is burning brightly for baking the cake."

Gustave started for the grocery store, but he had not gone very far on the way when he met his friend Max, who had a new velocipede, painted red. Max called to Gustave:

"You may ride my velocipede as much as you like," he said. "We will take turns."

Gustave stopped. He had no velocipede of his own. He could imagine himself riding on Max's velocipede, the wheels spinning around so fast as he played that he was a fire engine chief, or an automobile racer, or a chariot driver in a circus. But it was only a second that Gustave stopped. His new shoes would not let him stay any longer. On they raced toward the grocery store, carrying Gustave almost as fast as Max's velocipede could go. He called back to Max:

"I can't stop, now. I must fetch my mother a pat of butter by the time that the fire is ready for the cake."

That was all Gustave said. He did not tell him about the wonder shoes for that was a secret.

When he came back that way with the butter, Max was still out at play.

"I will race with you as far as my gate," Gustave said to Max.

"But I shall beat you because I am riding my velocipede and can race on wheels while you will have to race on foot," said Max.

But Gustave was off like an arrow and although Max worked the pedals of his new velocipede as fast as he could, he was not able to win the race. Gustave reached his gate before Max on his velocipede did.

"How did you go so fast?" asked Max.

"I have new shoes," said Gustave, but still he did not tell the secret of their wonder.

"I should like to have a pair just like them," said Max, who was often late for school and seldom able to do an errand for his mother promptly.

"I will ask the old shoemaker if he has any more shoes like mine, Max," Gustave said. So, after he had given his mother the pat of butter, which was exactly in time, he went back to the shop of the old shoemaker.

"My friend, Max, wants a pair of wonder shoes like mine," Gustave said. "Have you any more?" he asked.

The old shoemaker smiled, and chuckled, and laughed, until his spectacles nearly dropped off.

"More wonder shoes?" he said. "Why any little boy may have a pair if he wants them. It all depends upon the boy himself whether or not he has wonder shoes."

THE EMPEROR'S NEW CLOTHES

Many years ago there lived an Emperor who was so exceedingly fond of fine new clothes that he spent all his money on rich garments. He did not care for his soldiers, nor for the theatre, nor for driving about, except for the purpose of showing his new clothes.

He had a dress for every hour of the day, and just as they say of a king, "He is in Council," they always said of him, "The Emperor is in his Wardrobe."

Well, the great town in which he lived was very busy. Every day a number of strangers arrived.

One day two rogues came along, saying they were weavers, and that they knew how to weave the finest stuff one could imagine. Not only, said they, were the colors and designs exceedingly beautiful, but the clothes that were made of their material had the wonderful quality of being invisible to everybody who was either unfit for his position, or was extraordinarily stupid.

"They must be splendid clothes," thought the Emperor; "by wearing them I could easily discover what persons in my kingdom are unfit for their posts.

I could distinguish the wise from the stupid. I must have that stuff woven for me at once!" So he gave the two rogues a large sum of money, in order that they might begin their work without delay.

The rogues put up two looms, and pretended to be working, but they had nothing at all in the frames. Again and again they demanded the finest silks and the most magnificent gold thread, but they put it all in their own pockets, and worked at their empty looms late into the night.

"Now, I should like to know how far they have got on with that stuff," thought the Emperor; but he felt quite uncomfortable when he remembered that those who were stupid or unfit for their positions could not see it. He did not think for a moment that he had anything to fear for himself; but, nevertheless, he would rather send somebody else first to see how the stuff was getting on.

Everybody in the town knew what a remarkable quality the stuff possessed, and each was anxious to see how bad or stupid his neighbors were.

"I will send my honest old minister to the weavers," thought the Emperor; "he can judge best how the stuff looks, for he is intelligent, and no one is better fit for his office than he."

So the clever old minister went out into the hall, where the two rogues were sitting at work at their empty looms.

"Goodness me!" he thought, and opened his eyes wide; "I cannot see anything," but he did not say so. Both of the rogues begged him to be so kind as to step nearer, and asked him if it was not a pretty design, and were not the colors beautiful, and they pointed to the empty looms.

But the poor old minister kept on opening his eyes wider and wider: he could not see anything for there was nothing there.

"Goodness me!" he thought; "am I really stupid? I never thought so, and nobody must know it. Am I really unfit for my office? No; I must certainly not tell anybody that I cannot see the stuff."

"Well, what do you think of it?" asked the one who was weaving.

"Oh, it is beautiful! Most magnificent!" replied the old minister, and looked through his spectacles. "What a pattern! and what colors! Yes, I must tell the Emperor that I like it very much indeed."

"Ah! we are very glad of that," said both weavers, and then they described the colors, and explained the strange patterns.

The old minister listened attentively, so as to be able to repeat it all when he returned to the Emperor, and this he did.

The rogues now asked for more money, and for more silk and gold thread, which they required for weaving. They put everything into their pockets, and not a thread went on the frames, but nevertheless they continued to work at the empty looms.

Soon afterward the Emperor sent another clever statesman to see how the weaving was getting on, and whether the stuff was nearly ready. The same thing happened to him as to the minister; he looked and looked, but as there was nothing on the empty frames, he could not see anything.

"Now, is not that a beautiful piece of stuff?" said both rogues, and described the beauty of the pattern, which did not exist at all.

"I am not stupid," thought the statesman, "so it must be that I am unfit for the high position I hold; that is very strange, but I must not let anybody notice it." So he praised the piece of stuff which he could not see, and said how pleased he was with the beautiful colors and the pretty pattern.

"Oh! it is really magnificent!" he said to the Emperor.

All the people in the town were talking about the beautiful stuff, and the Emperor himself wished to see it while it was still on the loom. With a whole suite of chosen courtiers, among whom were the two honest old statesmen who had been there before, the Emperor went to the two cunning rogues, who were now weaving as fast as they could, but without thread or shuttle.

"Well! is it not magnificent?" cried the two clever statesmen; "does your majesty recognize how beautiful is the pattern, how charming the colors?"

and they pointed to the empty looms, for they thought that the others could see the stuff.

"What?" thought the Emperor; "I cannot see anything; this is terrible! Am I stupid; or am I not fit to be Emperor? This would be the most dreadful thing that could happen to me! Yes, it is very beautiful," he said at last; "we give our highest approbation!" and he nodded as if he were quite satisfied, and gazed at the empty looms.

He would not say that he saw nothing, and the whole of his suite looked and looked; but, like the others, they were unable to see anything. So they said, just like the Emperor, "Yes, it is very pretty," and they advised him to have some clothes made from this magnificent stuff, and to wear them for the first time at the great procession that was about to take place. "It is magnificent! beautiful! excellent!" they said one to another, and they were all so exceedingly pleased with it that the Emperor gave the two rogues a decoration to be worn in the button-hole, and the title "Imperial Weavers."

The rogues worked throughout the whole of the night preceding the day of the procession, and had over sixteen candles alight, so that people should see how busy they were in preparing the Emperor's new clothes.

They pretended to take the stuff off the looms, cut it in the air with great scissors, and sewed with needles without thread, and at last they said:

"See! now the clothes are ready!"

The Emperor, followed by his most distinguished courtiers, came in person, and the rogues lifted their arms up in the air, just as if they held something, and said, "See! here are the trousers, here is the coat, here is the cloak," and so forth. "It is as light as a cobweb; one might imagine one had nothing on, but that is just the beauty of it!"

"Yes," said all the courtiers; but they could not see anything, because there was nothing.

"Will your imperial highness condescend to undress?" said the rogues; "we will then attire your majesty in the new clothes, here in front of the mirror."

"Oh! how well they look! how beautifully they fit!" said every one; "what a pattern! what colors! It is indeed a magnificent dress."

"They are standing outside with the canopy which is to be carried over your majesty in the procession," announced the Master of Ceremonies.

"Well, I am ready," said the Emperor. "Does it not fit me well!" and he turned again to the mirror, for he wanted it to appear that he was admiring his rich costume.

The chamberlains who were to carry the train fumbled with their hands on the floor just as if they were holding the train up; they raised their hands in the air, but dared not let any body notice that they saw nothing; and so the Emperor went in procession beneath the magnificent canopy, and all the people in the street and at the windows said: "Oh! how beautiful the Emperor's new clothes are; what a splendid train, and how well everything fits!"

No one would admit that he could see nothing, for that would have shown that he was either unfit for his post or very stupid. None of the Emperor's costumes had ever been so much admired.

"But he has no robe on at all!" said a little child.

"Just hear the voice of the innocent," said his father, and one whispered to the other what the child had said.

"He has no robe on," cried the whole of the people at last; and the Emperor shivered, for it seemed to him that they were right.

But he thought to himself, "I must go through with the procession," and he walked with even greater dignity than before; and the chamberlains followed, carrying the train which did not exist at all.

HOW PRIMROSE WENT TO THE PARTY

The Prince who lived in the great white castle at the top of the green hill was to give a party, and he had invited the children from the village to come.

For days there had been talk of little else at the cottage doorsteps, and in the market place. Oh, the children all knew how wonderful a party at the

Prince's castle would be. The doors would be thrown wide open; in all the rooms there would be rose trees of every kind and color; birds would sing in golden cages; and each child would be given a feast and precious gifts.

There was something else, though, that the children knew. One must be dressed in a fitting way to appear at the castle of the Prince. Each child knew that he or she must appear in the best that they had to wear.

Well, that was easily arranged. They nearly all had ribbons, and there were bits of fine lace laid away in the home chests that could trim their frocks. Pieces of velvet were to be had and the village tailor was busy, night and day, making ruffled shirts and fine suits for the boys, while the mothers stitched and embroidered for the girls.

But when their party clothes were made, another thought came to the children. They should, themselves, carry gifts to the Prince.

This, also, was arranged. A bit of old carving from this cottage, an old silver cup from that shelf, a basket of rare fruits from this fertile orchard. These were good gifts.

So, at last, the children started up the hill to the castle. All were ready to meet the Prince, they felt sure, except Primrose; she walked apart from the others for she had no party dress, and no gift to carry.

She was named Primrose because she made a poor, bare little hut on the edge of the forest bright, just as a wild flower makes a waste spot beautiful. In all her life Primrose had never been to a party, and now she was invited with the others. But her feet were bare, and her little brown dress was torn, and she had no hat to cover her wind-blown, yellow hair.

As they went up the hill, the children passed a poor fagot gatherer, bending under her great bundle.

"Off a pleasuring, with little thought for others," the old woman mumbled to herself, but Primrose stole up to her side and slipped one soft little hand in the woman's hard, care-worn one.

"I will carry half your fagots for you to the turn of the road," she said. And she did, with the old woman's blessing on her sunny head at the turn.

Farther on, the children passed a young thrush that had fallen out of its nest and was crying beside the road. The mother bird cried, too. It was as if she said,

"You have no thought of my trouble."

But Primrose lifted the bird in her two hands and scrambled through the bushes until she had found its nest and put it safely in. The branches tore her dress that had been ragged before, but the mother thrush sang like a flute to have her little one back.

Just outside the castle gates, there was a blind boy seated, asking alms. When the other children passed him, laughing and chattering of all that they saw, tears fell down the cheeks of the little blind boy, for he had not been able to see for a long, long time. The others did not notice him, but Primrose stopped beside him and put her hands softly on his eyes. Then she picked a wild rose that grew beside the road and put it close to his face. He could feel its soft petals, and smell its perfume, and it made him smile.

Then Primrose hurried through the castle gates and up to the doors. They were about to be closed. The children had crowded in.

"There is no one else to come," the children shouted.

Then they added, "There is no other child except Primrose and she has no dress for a party and no gift for you, great Prince."

But the Prince, his kind eyes looking beyond them, and his arms outstretched, asked,

"What child, then, do I see coming in so wonderful a dress and carrying a precious gift in her hand?"

The children turned to look. They saw a little girl who wore a crown; it was the fagot bearer's blessing that had set it upon her head. Her dress was of wonderful gold lace; each rag had been turned to gold when she helped the little lost bird. In her hand she carried a clear, white jewel; her gift for the Prince; it was a tear she had taken from the little blind boy's face.

"Why, that is Primrose," the children told the Prince.

FOOD

THE PRINCE WHO WASN'T HUNGRY

Once upon a time there was a little Prince who had very little to do, and so he thought a great deal about eating. All the grown-up people in the castle were most anxious to have the little Prince grow up to be a fine, strong King. So they, too, thought a great deal about what the Prince should eat. The Queen made out long lists of good things for his meals. The Court Chancellor bought food, himself, in town so as to be sure that it would be fresh. The Court Cook was busy boiling, and broiling, and simmering, and tasting for the little Prince almost all day long. While the Court Ladies in Waiting served the little Prince's meals in the most dainty ways: sometimes on rosebud china, and sometimes in gold bowls, and always with silver spoons.

Such delicious foods as they were! No child, but a Prince, had ever tasted them.

There were wheat cakes made from only golden wheat, and served with honey from the wild bees' combs. There were eggs that a tiny bantam hen had laid, made into an omelette with very rare herbs from the castle kitchen garden. There were tarts filled with wild strawberries or black cherries, which every one knows are the nicest strawberries and cherries of all. There were such strange, sweet dishes as violet jelly, and rose-leaf jam, and clover preserve, very good indeed for supper, spread on sugar wafers.

At first the little Prince had an excellent appetite for all these good things. He looked forward so to his meals that he thought very little about running and playing with the castle pages. Instead, he spent ever so much time watching the clock, and he made up a new timetable for himself.

"Half past breakfast, it is now!" the little Prince would say, or, "A quarter before dinner," or, "Ten minutes of supper." And the Prince grew so fat that he looked like a little stuffed pig.

But after a while, the Prince lost his appetite. None of the rare foods that they gave him tasted as delicious as they had before. He began asking for things to eat that no one could give him; a blue apple, or a mug of dew, or a pat of butter made of buttercups.

"What shall we do about it?" all the people in the castle said, and the Queen cried, and the Court Cook wrung his hands. The little Prince would eat nothing else, and they were afraid that he would starve.

Then the little Prince asked them for the best food in the world, and would have no other. He had eaten what every one thought was the best, so they did not know what to do. One day they missed the little Prince. He had gone down into the village to try and find, for himself, the best food in the world.

He asked every one whom he met about it. Every one knew from his velvet suit and his buckled shoes that he was the Prince, so they all tried to feed him.

"Now, I have the best food in the world, a nicely roasted chicken," said the innkeeper.

"Oh, no, I have eaten roasted chicken and I am tired of it, thank you," said the Prince.

"I am sure that I have the best food in the world," said the baker, "a frosted plum cake."

"Oh, no, I have eaten frosted plum cake, and I am tired of it, thank you," said the Prince.

"Of course I have the best food in the world, chocolate ice cream," said the sweets man.

"Oh, no, I have eaten chocolate ice cream and I am tired of it, thank you," said the Prince.

So he went this way and that way, but he could not find anything that he wanted to eat.

When it was late in the afternoon he came to the woods and there he met a little boy of his own age, chopping down small trees. The boy's cheeks were rosy, and his eyes were bright. His arms, swinging the shiny hatchet, were tough with strong muscles. He looked as if he had eaten good food all his life, so the little Prince spoke to him.

"Have you any of the best food in the world?" he asked.

"Oh, yes; right here in my pocket," said the boy.

"May I have some?" begged the little Prince.

"Yes, indeed," said the boy, "if you will help me with my chopping first. I am not going to eat my supper until I have finished my work."

So the little Prince took the hatchet and chopped, while the boy tied the wood into bundles and gathered up the chips. The air was crisp and sweet, and the work made the little Prince's blood flow fast and warm. He liked it very much indeed, so he kept on chopping until his arms ached and he had to sit down on a stump to rest.

"Now we will eat," said the boy, and he pulled a piece of strange, dark food from his pocket. He broke it in two and gave half to the Prince who ate it in hungry mouthfuls.

It tasted better than anything he had ever eaten before!

"It is the best food in the world. Thank you," said the little Prince. "I shall see that you are made a page, and I will take back part of this food to share with my mother, the Queen."

But the Queen and all the other people were very much surprised at what the little Prince brought them.

It was a piece of brown bread and butter!

THE FIELD

The field was small, and full of stones, and barren. Although it lay beside a much travelled road and not far from the town, no one had noticed it except to say how useless it was.

"It would take a great deal of time to cultivate that field," the farmer said as he drove by in the fall with his team full of ripe vegetables and fruit for market. He had bought a farm that was ploughed and planted. There had been no stones for him to dig out and take away.

"That would be a fine field to play in," said the children as they passed by on their way to school, "only it is too rough. It would hurt our feet."

"If only something could be raised in the field," said the people who had houses close by. "Then we should be sure of having food for the winter."

But no one paid any further attention to the field.

There was a secret about it, though.

The field was alive. Deep down in its earth, under its thick clods and heavy stones, the field had a great wish to grow. And to grow, the field must be clean, so it called to Mother Nature for help. Mother Nature spoke to her winds about it.

"Four Winds," she said, "will you sweep the field clean, and so help it to grow?"

The winds heard Mother Nature calling and they got out their four brooms and swept the field as clean as they could. But that was not enough. The field must be rich as well as clean before it could grow. So the field called once more to Mother Nature, and Mother Nature spoke to her trees.

"Trees of the roadside," she said, "will you give your leaves to cover the field, and lose their beautiful colors, and become loam? The four winds have swept the field clean, but it must be rich before it can grow."

The trees heard Mother Nature calling, and they gave all their leaves to the field. But that was not enough. The field must be dug, as well as enriched and cleaned, before it could grow.

So the field called a third time to Mother Nature, and Mother Nature spoke to her children, the earth worms.

"Earth Worms," she said, "will you creep and dig underneath the field and turn up the earth in furrows? The four winds have swept the earth clean, and the trees have given their leaves to make it rich, but it must be dug before it can grow."

Although the earth worms are very small, they heard Mother Nature calling. They crept down under the earth and began working together to dig the field. Wherever they found rich earth they threw it up to take the place of the fallow. But their work was not enough. The field must be planted, as well as dug and enriched and cleaned, before it could grow. So the field called again to Mother Nature, and Mother Nature spoke to her children in feathers and soft coats.

"Birds and Four-Footed Children in soft coats," she said, "will you bring seeds and scatter them over the field? The four winds have swept it clean, and the trees have given their leaves to make it rich. The earth worms have dug the field, but it must be planted before it can grow."

Then the birds brought all kinds of seeds in their feathers, and the squirrels and the chipmunks and the sheep and the cattle passing through brought seeds in their soft coats and scattered them over the field. But this was not enough. The field must be nourished as well as planted, and dug, and enriched, and cleaned before it could grow. So the field called again to Mother Nature, and Mother Nature spoke to the sky.

"Sky," she said, "will you send rain and sun to the fields? The four winds have swept it clean, and the trees have given their leaves to make it rich. The earth worms have dug the field, and my children in feathers and soft coats have planted it, but it must be nourished before it can grow."

So the sky sent down spring rains and golden sunshine to the field, and the field's great wish began to come true. Where there had been only rough clods and between the heavy stones the field began to grow. The seeds of green grass, and of bright flowers, and of many different kinds of grain sprouted and pushed up through the earth. An apple seed sent up a shoot that would be an apple tree some day. An acorn sent up a tiny oak tree that would grow and grow until it was large enough to be cut for the beams of a house or the sides of a ship. But that was not enough. The field must be tended as well as nourished, and planted, and dug, and enriched, and cleaned before its great wish could really come true. So the field called for the last time to Mother Nature, and Mother Nature spoke to her humble child, the toad.

"Toad," she said, "will you tend the field? The four winds have swept it, and the trees have given their leaves to make it rich. The earth worms have dug the field, and my children in feathers and soft coats have planted it. The sky has sent rain and sun to nourish it, but it must be guarded from enemies before it can grow."

So the toad and all his brothers, who had been hiding beneath the stones of the field that they might not be killed, came out, and tended the field. They ate the insects and other creatures that would have destroyed the sprouts, and so the field grew.

It lay in the sunshine, bright with flowers, and green with the sprouts of growing food and trees.

"A fertile field!" said the farmer. "I shall help it to grow."

"The field is alive!" cried the children. "We can go in it and help the farmer."

"The field is rich!" said all the people who lived near by. "It is growing, and will help us to live."

And the field was cleaned, and enriched, and ploughed, and planted, and nourished, and tended each year by the hands of children and men. They took away the clods and the stones, for they had found out the secret hidden underneath. The field was alive, and it had a great wish to grow.

THE MAGIC SAUCEPAN

A long time ago, in the days of the fairies and other little folk, there lived a housewife who was very stingy indeed. She thought only of her own cupboard and meals, and never of the needs of her neighbors. When she did give alms it was a dry loaf or a scraped bone for which she had no use, and she looked for great reward because she gave even these.

She lived in the country, not far from the hills where the little Hillmen stayed. The Hillmen were fairy folk, kin to the elves and in appearance somewhat like the brownies. They made their homes in the trunks of old trees or in the hollows of the hills, gathering nuts, and grains, and such fruits as the farmers dropped at the time of harvesting. They were generous, kind little folk and couldn't abide meanness.

One day a Hillman came down and knocked at the door of the housewife. When her maid-servant opened it a crack, he took off his little green cap politely and told her his errand.

"We're giving a christening party on the hill to-night, good mother," the Hillman said, "and we need an extra saucepan, for all of ours are in use. Will you lend us one?"

"Shall I loan one of our saucepans to the Hillman, mistress?" the maid-servant asked.

"Oh, yes, I suppose it is wiser to be neighborly with them," the housewife replied.

So the maid-servant went over to the side of the kitchen where the pots hung on the wall to get a saucepan down. There was a fine supply to choose from, large and small, polished copper and brass, iron, and shining tin. But just as the maid-servant put out her hand to take one of their best saucepans, the housewife whispered to her.

"Not that one!" she said. "Give him the old one that leaks, and hangs there at the end. The Hillmen are tidy little folk and very nimble with a job of tinkering. They'll have to mend it before they use it and so it will come home whole. We can oblige the Fairy Folk and save sixpence at the same time."

The maid-servant was sorry to do her mistress's bidding, for it was the oldest and blackest saucepan of all, hung there to wait for the next time when the tinker stopped at the house. She gave it to the little Hillman, though, who thanked her and went off with the leaky saucepan hung over his back.

One morning, not long after that, they found the saucepan, returned, on the doorstep. It was neatly mended, ready for use.

When it was supper time, the maid-servant filled the pan with milk and set it over the fire to heat it for the children's supper. She had scarcely done this, though, when there was a great sizzling and sputtering, and the milk was burned so badly that not even the pigs would eat it.

"Look what you have done!" the housewife said, scolding the maid-servant. "You have ruined a quart of rich milk with your carelessness, a whole quart of milk with the cream, all gone at once!"

"And that's twopence!" said a shrill, whining voice that seemed to come from the chimney.

They went to the door and looked up on the roof, and they looked up the chimney, but they could see no one. At last they decided that it must have been the wind they had heard; and the housewife, herself, filled the saucepan with milk once more and set it over the fire. She only turned around, though, when the milk boiled over. Again, it was just as burned and spoiled as it had been before.

"Well, this is no fault of mine," the housewife said. "The saucepan must be dirty; but now there are two quarts of rich milk with the cream, all wasted."

"And that's fourpence!" said the strange voice, speaking again, and this time it seemed to come from out of the fire itself.

They looked behind the bellows and back of the chimney, but they could see no one. They made up their minds at last that it must have been the creaking of the fire logs that they had heard. The housewife washed, and scrubbed, and scoured the saucepan, and then she filled it for a third time with all the milk that she had left. She set it for the third time over the fire, and both she and the maid-servant watched it to see that nothing happened to it.

Then, before their very eyes, the milk burned and boiled over for a third time. It was hopelessly spoiled. The housewife began to cry at the waste. "I never had anything like this befall me in my life!" she bemoaned. "I have wasted three quarts of milk for one meal!"

"And that's sixpence," said the voice that seemed now to be right at her elbow. "You didn't save the price of the tinkering after all."

She turned and there was the Hillman, standing right beside her, his little green cap in his hand, and laughing with all his might. Before she could catch him, he was off and out through the kitchen door.

TOYS

THE TOP THAT COULD SING

Once upon a time there was a little painted tin top that lay in a toy shop window. It was a most beautiful tin top with a painted stripe of red, and a painted stripe of yellow, and a painted stripe of green. The tin of which it was made was as bright and shining as silver, and it had one little pointed toe upon which it could dance most merrily when its string was unwound.

But more wonderful than the colors of the tin top, or the shine of it, or its one little tin toe, was its voice. The very moment that it began to dance it began, too, to sing in a sweet, cheerful humming kind of way. And it kept on singing as long as it kept on dancing, and its voice was never less sweet or less cheerful.

One day Gerald came to the toy shop with his mother because it was his birthday and he was to select a new toy. A boy who is to have a new toy should smile, but Gerald frowned. He had so many toys at home that he could not decide which new one to choose.

"Will you have a box of toy soldiers?" asked his mother.

"No, I'm tired of soldiers," Gerald said crossly.

"Will you have a new ball?" asked the toy man.

"I don't want any more balls," Gerald replied quite crossly.

"Oh, see this game!" said his mother.

"Games are stupid," Gerald answered most crossly.

"Then, listen!" said the toy man taking the little tin top from its place, winding it up, pulling off the string and then setting it down upon the floor. Away danced the bright little top upon its one little tin toe and as it danced it sang its sweet, cheerful, humming song.

Gerald listened. Then the ugly frown left his face and in its place there came a happy smile. He clapped his hands as the little tin top circled, and whirled, and tripped, and hopped around his feet.

"May I buy the top that sings?" he asked and his mother said that he might. So they paid a bright ten cent piece for it and the toy man put the little tin top into Gerald's hands. As they left the toy shop, Gerald still smiled and he hopped along beside his mother as he remembered how the little tin top had hopped. And his mother made up a song about it that they hummed softly together:

"To and fro, on its little tin toe,Singing and dancing the top will go.Spinning and singing it seems to say,'Children should always be glad and gay.'"

So they went on until they came to a big building that was a hospital, and at one of the front windows a sick-a-bed child was propped up on pillows and looking out. Gerald looked in; then he motioned for the nurse who stood near to open the window, and he wound the little tin top and started it spinning on the sidewalk. It could spin and sing indoors or outdoors. Round and round it danced and it seemed to be saying:

"To and fro on my little tin toe,Singing and spinning, oh, see me go!This is the song that I sing to-day,'Children should always be glad and gay.'"

The sick-a-bed child watched the little tin top, its whirling colors looking like a rainbow in the sunlight. She listened to its sweet, cheerful, humming song. Then her sick-a-bed, tired face changed to a happy, smiling face, and she clapped her hands and laughed so loudly that Gerald could hear her, for she had heard what the little tin top sang.

Then they went on a little farther and they came to a boy who sold newspapers on the street corner. He had just seen another boy who sold newspapers coming and he had decided to have a fight with him, for he did not want him to sell his papers on that corner. An ugly frown covered his face, but suddenly he saw Gerald with his little top in his hands.

"Can you spin it?" he asked of Gerald.

"Watch and see!" Gerald answered.

So Gerald wound the little tin top and started it spinning by the newsboy's pile of papers. It could spin and sing anywhere, even on a street curbing. Round and round it danced, and it seemed to be saying again:

"To and fro on my little tin toe,Singing and spinning, oh, see me go!This is the song that I sing to-day,'Children should always be glad and gay.'"

The newsboy listened to the sweet, cheerful humming song of the little tin top. Then he, too, laughed and he motioned to the other newsboy to come and see the top.

"Put your papers down here by mine," he said as Gerald picked up the top and started on.

They were almost home now, and just as they reached their own street he heard the voices of his two friends, Peter and Polly, and they were very loud, cross voices indeed.

"It's my turn to ride in the cart," shouted Peter.

"No, it's my turn to ride in the cart!" shouted Polly.

"Peter and Polly, look; see what I have for my birthday," said Gerald. Then Gerald wound the little tin top and started it spinning in front of Peter and Polly. It could sing and spin anywhere, even in front of a little quarreling brother and sister. Round and round it whirled, and it seemed to be saying once again:

"To and fro on my little tin toe,Singing and spinning, oh, see me go!This is the song that I sing to-day,'Children should always be glad and gay.'"

"Oh, the pretty top!" shouted Peter and Polly as they listened to its sweet, cheerful, humming song. Then Peter said to Polly:

"It's your turn to ride in the cart, Polly."

But Polly said to Peter: "Oh, no, it's your turn to ride in the cart, Peter."

And that was the wonderful secret of the little tin top; wherever it took its spinning, singing way it made little children glad and gay.

THE MONEY PIG

In the nursery a number of toys lay strewn about. High up, on the cupboard, stood the money box, made of clay in the shape of a little pig. The pig had by nature a slit in his back, and this slit had been so enlarged with a knife that whole silver dollars could slip through. Indeed, two dollar pieces had slipped into the box beside a number of pennies. The money pig was stuffed so full that he could no longer rattle, and that is the highest point of perfection a money pig can attain.

There he stood upon the cupboard, high and lofty, looking down upon everything else in the room. He knew very well that what he had in his stomach would have bought all the toys.

The others thought of that, too, even if they did not say it, for there were many other things to speak of. One of the drawers was half pulled out and there lay a great handsome doll, although she was somewhat old, and her neck had been mended. She looked out and said,

"Now we'll play at being men and women."

And then there was a general uproar. Even the framed pictures on the wall turned round to show that they had a wrong side; but that was not because they objected.

It was late at night. The moon shone through the window frames and afforded the most economical light. The game was now to begin and all, even the children's go-cart, which certainly belonged to the coarser playthings, were invited to take part in the fun.

"Each of us has his own peculiar value," said the go-cart. "We cannot all be noblemen. There must be some who work."

The money pig was the only one of the toys who received a written invitation, for he was of high standing and great pride, and they were afraid he would not accept a verbal invitation. Indeed he did not answer to say whether he would come, nor did he come. They understood that if he were to take a part, he must enjoy the sport from his own home. The others must arrange things accordingly, and so they did.

The little toy theatre was set up in such a way that the money pig could look directly in. They wanted to begin with a play, and afterward there was to be a party and a little conversation among themselves. They began with this latter part immediately. The rocking horse talked about training and racing, and the go-cart of railways and steam power, for all this belonged to their professions and it was quite right that they should speak of it.

The toy clock talked politics—tick—tick—and knew what was the time of day, although it was whispered that he did not go correctly. The little boy's cane stood there, stiff and straight, for he was conceited about his brass tip and his silver handle. On the sofa lay two embroidered cushions, pretty and stupid.

And then the play began.

They all sat and looked on. The play was not very good, but the actors did their part. These were little card-board figures who turned their painted side to the audience. They were so made that they should only be looked at from that side, and not from the other. They all played wonderfully well, coming out beyond the footlights because the wires were a little too long, but that only helped them to come out the more.

The worsted doll enjoyed the play so much that she became quite exhausted from excitement. She laughed so hard that she burst at the darned place in her neck. And the money pig was so enchanted in his way that he decided to do something for one of the players in his will.

It was a great deal of fun. They gave up all thoughts of having tea, and just played and talked together. That was what they called playing at being men and women, and there was nothing wrong in it for they were only playing. Each one thought, however, of what the money pig might think; and the money pig thought of his own riches and of making his will. This seemed to him a long way farther on.

When might it come to pass? Certainly far sooner than was expected.

Crack! The money pig fell from the cupboard—fell to the floor and was broken to pieces. All the money came out. The pennies hopped and danced about in a comical fashion; the little ones spun around like tops, and the bigger coins rolled away, particularly one great silver dollar that wanted to go out into the world. It came out into the world and so did they all.

And the pieces of the money pig were put into the dustbin. The next day a new money pig was standing on the cupboard. It had not a penny in its stomach and so it could not rattle, and in this it was like the other. And that was a beginning—and with that we will make an end.

THE GIANT'S PLAYTHING

Long ago, giants lived among the lonely mountains. Now there was a great castle, called Burg Niedeck, that stood on top of the highest mountain of Alsace, and here the most powerful of the giants lived with his wife and family. He had one child, named Freda.

Freda was as tall as a church steeple. She was a curious child, and very fond of prying about and looking at things which she had been told to leave alone. She was allowed to roam all about the mountains, and to play in the woods and forest, but she was not allowed to go down into the valley where the little people lived.

These little peasants tilled the ground, and planted corn and wheat and barley, and pruned their vines, and dug ditches, things the giants could not do. And the giants lived by taking what the little people raised. Now, it was said that the first time a peasant found his way up into Burg Niedeck it would be the end of the giants. But Burg Niedeck was very high and difficult to reach and no peasant had ever thought of trying to get there.

One day Freda was playing outside the castle gates in the sunshine. The valley looked so cool and green and shady that, seeing no one about, she went down the mountain-side to find out what was below.

Presently she saw, in a field in which she was standing, a peasant plowing. He had two horses and the iron of the plow shone and glistened.

With a cry of delight Freda knelt down.

"What a dear little toy!" she said. "I will take it home to play with."

Spreading out her handkerchief on the ground, she carefully lifted the plow and the horses and the poor peasant and set them down in the middle. Then, taking the corners of the handkerchief in her hand, she ran up the mountain-side, skipping and jumping for pleasure. It was like the coming of an earthquake.

Her father met her at the gate.

"Well, little one," he said, "what is pleasing you so?"

"Look!" said Freda, spreading out her handkerchief. "I have found a most wonderful new toy." And she lifted out the plow and the peasant.

The old giant frowned, and shook his head in anger.

"What have you done, thoughtless one?" he stormed. "That is no toy. Have you not heard that as soon as a peasant comes to Burg Niedeck there will be an end of the giants forever? Take it back instantly to the valley and perhaps the spell will not break."

Sadly Freda took the plow and the horses and the peasant back and set them in the field. But it was too late. That night all the giants disappeared, and in the morning Burg Niedeck stood in ruins. And to this day no giant has ever been seen there.

TRADE LIFE

THE HOLIDAY

The old clock that hung in the tower of the town hall struck one.

It was dark, except for a few twinkling stars like bright eyes in the night sky. All the town was asleep. It was cold, and white snow lay over every thing. But as the clock struck one, the baker awoke and went down to his kitchen to light his ovens. It was time for the fire to glow and burn for his baking when the clock struck one o'clock.

Two struck the clock in the tower of the town hall.

As the clock struck two the baker put on his white apron and rolled up his sleeves. He bent over his great mixing bowl and began kneading the dough and shaping the loaves of bread that were to be baked in the oven.

It was time at two o'clock for the loaves of bread to go into the oven to bake in the fire that glowed and burned so early in the morning.

Three struck the clock in the tower of the town hall.

The dairyman poured rich milk into his shining bottles and packed them into the milkman's wagon. It was still dark, although the stars were not so bright and the sky was just beginning to be streaked with pink. It was very cold, but the dairyman knew that it was time at three o'clock to measure the milk that must go to town for the children to drink as they ate the bread that the baker had mixed and baked.

Four struck the clock in the old town hall. Now the sky was light enough for the milkman's team to start out, driving over the hard, frosty roads. No other people were out, but the milkman knew that he must start to town at four o'clock and begin delivering his milk that the dairyman had measured so early in the morning. The children must have it to drink as they ate the bread that the baker had mixed at two, and baked in the fire that had been lighted at one o'clock.

Five struck the clock in the town hall. A wintry wind blew out of the east. It bit the nose and ears of the baker's boy who started out with a basket of fresh loaves of bread on his arm for delivering at the kitchen doors. He ran and whistled to try and keep warm. He did not stop to think of anything, though, except that five o'clock was time to deliver a loaf of bread at every house where the milkman had left a bottle of milk.

Six struck the clock in the town hall.

Jack's mother came downstairs and raised the house curtains to let in the first sunshine, and then she put on her apron to begin the work of the day. She spread a clean cloth over the table and laid the knives and forks and spoons, and set the cups and bowls and plates in their places. She knew that six o'clock was time to make the house ready for breakfast. The baker's boy had started at five, and the milkman had brought the milk at four. The dairyman had measured the milk at three for the children to drink when they ate the bread that the baker had mixed at two, and baked in the fire he had lighted at one.

Seven struck the clock in the town hall. The tea kettle on the kitchen stove sang. The sun shone in brightly, and Jack knew that it was time to get up. But Jack was sleepy. He pulled the blankets up over his nose and buried his head in his pillow so that he should not hear the sound of the clock. It was a holiday, and Jack had decided to do nothing but sleep and play.

Ting-a-ling; what was that? Jack jumped out of bed and into his clothes when he heard the loud ring at the house door. Then he heard his mother's voice.

"Good morning, Tom; you are out early, are you not? And here are all my groceries; the butter, and the sugar, and the fruit, and the eggs! Now I shall be able to make a cake to-day."

Jack knew who it was that had come through the cold, before he was up in the morning, with a basket of groceries. It was Tom, the grocer's boy.

Then Jack heard other sounds as he went downstairs and ate his breakfast. He heard the sound of the baker kneading his bread, and the drip of the milk as the dairyman measured it. He heard the rattle of the milkman's cart and the sound of the baker's boy whistling as he delivered his loaves in the cold. He saw Tom coming down the street again with his empty basket on his arm. He was going back to the grocery store for another load.

Jack put on his hat and coat and ran out.

"Wait, Tom!" he called, "I have a holiday and I'll help you deliver the groceries this morning."

NILS AND THE BEAR

Nils had been exploring the mining districts a whole day.

"I must try and climb up to earth again," he said at last, "otherwise, I fear my companions won't find me."

The boy was about to go up the mountain when he heard a gruff voice growl in his ear, "Who are you?"

He thought at first that he was facing a huge rock covered with brownish moss. Then he noticed that the rock had broad paws to walk with, a head, two eyes, and a growling mouth.

He could not pull himself together to answer, nor did the big bear appear to expect it of him, for he knocked him down, rolled him back and forth with his paws and nosed him. The bear seemed just about ready to swallow him when the boy had a thought. Quick as a flash he dug into his pocket and brought forth some matches, — his sole weapon of defence, — lighted one on his leather breeches, and thrust the burning match into the bear's open mouth.

Father Bear snorted when he smelled the sulphur, and with that the flame went out.

"Can you light many of those little blue roses?" asked Father Bear.

"I can light enough to put an end to the whole forest," replied the boy, for he thought that in this way he might scare Father Bear.

"Perhaps you could also set fire to houses and barns," said Father Bear.

"Oh, that would be nothing for me," boasted the boy.

"Good!" exclaimed the bear. "You shall render me a service. Now I'm very glad that I did not eat you!"

Father Bear carefully took Nils between his paws and climbed up from the pit. As soon as he was up, he speedily made for the woods. Then he ran along until he came to a hill at the edge of the forest. Here he lay in front of Nils, holding him securely between his forepaws.

"Now look down at that big noise-shop!" he commanded.

The great iron works, with many tall buildings, stood at the edge of the waterfall. High chimneys sent forth dark clouds of smoke, blasting furnaces blazed, and light shone from all the windows. Within, hammers and rolling mills were going with such force that the air rang with their clatter and boom. All about the workshops were immense coal sheds, great slag heaps, warehouses, wood piles, and tool sheds. Just beyond were long rows of workingmen's houses, as quiet as if they were asleep. The earth around them was black while the works, themselves, were sending out light and smoke, fire and sparks. It was the grandest sight the boy had ever seen.

"Could you set fire to a place like that?" Father Bear asked doubtfully.

The boy stood wedged between the beast's paws, thinking the only thing that might save him would be that the bear should have a high opinion of his power.

"It's all the same to me," he answered with a superior air. "Big or little, I can burn it down."

"Then I'll tell you something," said Father Bear.

"My forefathers lived in this region from the time that the forests first sprang up. From them I inherited hunting grounds and pastures, lairs and retreats. In the beginning I wasn't much troubled by the human kind. They dug in the mountains and picked up a little ore down here by the rapids. They had a forge and a furnace, but the hammer sounded only a few hours each day, and the furnace was not fired more than two moons at a stretch.

"But these last years, since they have built this noise-shop, there is racket day and night. I thought I should have to move away, but now I have discovered a better way."

Father Bear took Nils up again and lumbered down the hill. He walked fearlessly between the workshops, and climbed to the top of a slag heap.

There he sat up on his haunches and held the boy up high between his paws.

"Try to look into the shop," he said.

The boy saw a workman take a short, thick bar of iron at white heat from a furnace opening, and place it under a roller that flattened and extended it. Immediately another workman seized it and placed it beneath a heavier roller. Thus it was passed from roller to roller until, finally, it curled along the floor like a long red thread. Continuously fresh threads followed it like hissing snakes.

"I call that real man's work!" the boy said to himself.

Father Bear then let him have a peep at the forge, and he became more and more astonished as he saw how the blacksmiths handled iron and fire.

"Those men have no fear of heat and flames," he thought.

"They keep this up day after day," Father Bear said as he dropped wearily on the ground. "One gets tired of that kind of thing. I'm glad that at last I can put an end to it."

The boy was all of a shiver now.

"If you will set fire to the noise-shop, I'll spare your life," said Father Bear.

Just beyond them lay a pile of chips and shavings, and beside it was a wood pile that almost reached the coal shed. The coal shed extended over to the workshops, and if that once caught fire, the flames would soon fly over to the iron foundry. The walls would fall from the heat, and the machinery would be destroyed.

"Will you or won't you?" demanded Father Bear.

"You mustn't be so impatient," the boy said. "Let me think a moment."

"Very well," said Father Bear, tightening his hold on the boy.

They needed iron for everything, Nils knew. There was iron in the plough that broke up the field, and in the axe that felled the tree for building houses, in the scythe that mowed the grain, and in the knife that could be turned to all sorts of uses. There was iron in the horse's bit, and in the lock on the door, in the nails that held the furniture together, and in the sheathing that covered the roof. Iron covered the men-of-war that he had seen in the harbor, the locomotives steamed through the country on iron rails. The needle that had stitched the boy's coat was made of iron, the shears that clipped the sheep, and the kettle that cooked the food. The rifle which drove away wild beasts was made of iron. Father Bear was perfectly right. He knew that the coming of iron to the forest had given the human kind their mastery over the beasts.

"Will you or won't you?" demanded Father Bear.

The boy shrank back. He swept his hand across his forehead. He could see no way of escape, but this much he knew, he did not wish to do any harm to the iron which was useful to so many people in the land.

"I won't!" he said.

Father Bear squeezed him a little harder but said nothing.

"You'll not get me to destroy the ironworks," defied the boy. "The iron is so great a blessing that it will never do to harm it."

"Then of course you don't expect to be allowed to live very long," said the bear.

"No, I don't expect it," replied the boy, looking the bear straight in the eye.

Father Bear gripped him still harder. It hurt so that the boy could not keep the tears back, but he did not cry out or say a word.

"Very well, then," said Father Bear, raising his paw very slowly, hoping that the boy would give in at the last moment.

But just then the boy heard something click very close to them, and saw the muzzle of a rifle two paces away.

"Father Bear! Don't you hear the clicking of a trigger?" cried the boy. "Run, or you will be shot!"

Father Bear grew terribly hurried. He gave himself time, though, to pick up the boy and carry him along. As he ran, a couple of shots sounded; the bullets grazed his ears, but he escaped.

When Father Bear had run some distance into the woods, he paused and set Nils down on the ground.

"Thank you, little one," he said. "I dare say those bullets would have caught me if you hadn't been there. Now I want to do you a service in return. If you should ever meet with another bear, just say to him this — which I shall whisper to you — and he won't touch you."

Father Bear whispered a word or two into the boy's ear and then hurried away.

THE GIANT ENERGY AND THE FAIRY SKILL

Long, long ago, when there were giants to be seen, as they might be seen now if we only looked in the right place, there lived a young giant who was very strong and very willing, but who found it hard to get work to do.

The name of the giant was Energy, and he was so great and clumsy that people were afraid to trust their work to him.

If he were asked to put a bell in the church steeple, he would knock the steeple down before he finished the work. If he were sent to reach a broken weather vane, he would tear off part of the roof in his zeal. So, at last, people would not employ him and he went away to the mountains to sleep; but he could not rest, even though other giants were sleeping as still as great rocks under the shade of the trees.

Young Giant Energy could not sleep for he was too anxious to help in the world's work; and he went down into the valley, and begged so piteously for something to do that a good woman gave him a basket of china to carry home for her.

"This is child's play for me," said the giant as he set the basket down so hard that every bit of the china was broken.

"I wish a child had brought it for me," answered the woman, and the young giant went away sorrowful. He climbed the mountain and lay down to rest; but he could not stay there and do nothing, so he went back to the valley to look for work.

There he met the good woman. She had forgiven him for breaking her china, and had made up her mind to trust him again; so she gave him a pitcher of milk to carry home.

"Be quick in bringing it," she said, "lest it sour on the way."

The giant took the pitcher and made haste to run to the house; and he ran so fast that the milk was spilled and not a drop was left when he reached the good woman's house.

The good woman was sorry to see this, although she did not scold; and the giant went back to his mountain with a heavy heart.

Soon, however, he was back again, asking at every house:

"Isn't there something for me to do?" and again he met the good woman, who was here, there, and everywhere, carrying soup to the sick and food to the hungry.

When she met the young Giant Energy, her heart was full of love for him; and she told him to make haste to her house and fill her tubs with water, for the next day was wash day.

Then the giant made haste with mighty strides towards the good woman's house, where he found her great tubs; and, lifting them with ease, he carried them to the cistern and began to pump.

He pumped with such force and with so much delight, that the tubs were soon filled so full that they ran over, and when the good woman came home she found her yard as well as her tubs full of water.

The young giant had such a downcast look, that the good woman could not be angry with him; she only felt sorry for him.

"Go to the Fairy Skill, and learn," said the good woman, as she sat on the doorstep. "She will teach you, and you will be a help in the world after all."

"Oh! how can I go?" cried the giant, giving a jump that sent him over the tree tops, where he could see the little birds in their nests.

"Don't go so fast," said the good woman. "Stand still and listen! Go through the meadow, and count a hundred daffodils; then turn to your right, and walk until you find a mullein stalk that is bent. Notice the way it bends, and walk in that direction till you see a willow tree. Behind this willow runs a little stream. Cross the water by the way of the shining pebbles, and when you hear a strange bird singing you will see the fairy palace and the workmen where the Fairy Skill teaches her school. Go to her with my love and she will receive you."

The young giant thanked the good woman, stepped over the meadow fence, and counted the daffodils, "One, two, three," until he had counted a hundred. Then he turned to the right, and walked through the long grass to the bent mullein stalk, which pointed to the right, and after he had found the brook and crossed by way of the shining pebbles, he heard a strange bird singing, and saw among the trees the fairy palace.

He never could tell how it looked; but he thought it was made of sunshine, with the glimmer of green leaves reflected on it, and that it had the blue sky for a roof.

That was the palace; and at one side of it was the workshop, built of strong pines and oaks; and the giant heard the hum of wheels, and the noise of the fairy looms, where the fairies wove carpets of rainbow threads.

When the giant came to the door, the doorway stretched itself for him to pass through. He found Fairy Skill standing in the midst of the workers; and when he had given her the good woman's love, she received him kindly. Then she set him to work, bidding him sort a heap of tangled threads that lay in a corner like a great bunch of bright-colored flowers.

This was hard work for the giant's clumsy fingers, but he was very patient about it. The threads would break, and he got some of them into knots; but when Fairy Skill saw his work, she said:

"Very good for to-day;" and touching the threads with her wand, she changed them into a tangled heap again. The next day the giant tried again, and after that again, until every thread lay unbroken and untangled.

Then Fairy Skill said, "Well done," and led him to a loom and showed him how to weave.

This was harder work than the other had been; but Giant Energy was patient, although many times before his strip of carpet was woven the fairy touched it with her wand, and he had to begin over.

At last it was finished, and the giant thought it was the most beautiful carpet in the world.

Fairy Skill took him next to the potter's wheel, where cups and saucers were made out of clay; and the giant learned to be steady, to shape the cup as the wheel whirled round, and to take heed of his thumb, lest it slip.

The cups and saucers that were broken before he could make beautiful ones would have been enough to set the Queen's tea table!

Fairy Skill then took him to the goldsmith, and there he was taught to make chains and bracelets and necklaces; and after he had learned all these things, the fairy told him that she had three trials for him. Three pieces of work he must do; and if he did them well, he could go again into the world, for he would then be ready to be a helper there.

"The first task is to make a carpet," said Fairy Skill, "a carpet fit for a palace floor."

Giant Energy sprang to his loom, and made his silver shuttle glance under and over, under and over, weaving a most beautiful pattern.

As he wove, he thought of the way by which he had come; and his carpet became as green as the meadow grass, and lovely daffodils grew on it. When it was finished, it was almost as beautiful as a meadow full of flowers!

Then the fairy said that he must turn a cup fine enough for a king to use. And the giant made a cup in the shape of a flower; and when it was finished, he painted birds upon it with wings of gold. When she saw it, the fairy cried out with delight.

"One more trial before you go," she said. "Make me a chain that a queen might be glad to wear."

So Giant Energy worked by day and by night and made a chain of golden links; and in every link was a pearl as white as the shining pebbles in the brook. A queen might well have been proud to wear this chain.

After he had finished, Fairy Skill kissed him and blessed him, and sent him away to be a helper in the world, and she made him take with him the beautiful things which he had made, so that he might give them to the one he loved best.

The young giant crossed the brook, passed the willow, found the mullein stalk, and counted the daffodils.

When he had counted a hundred, he stepped over the meadow fence and came to the good woman's house.

The good woman was at home, so he went in at the door and spread the carpet on the floor, and the floor looked like the floor of a palace.

He set the cup on the table, and the table looked like the table of a king; and he hung the chain around the good woman's neck, and she was more beautiful than a queen.

And this is the way that young Giant Energy learned to be a helper in the world.

THE FARMER

THE FARM HOUSE

My name is Louisa Manners. I was seven years old on the first day of May. On the morning of that day, as soon as I awoke, I crept into mamma's bed, and said,

"Open your eyes, mamma, and look at me, for it is my birthday."

Then mamma told me I should ride in a post-chaise, and see my grandmamma. She lived at a farm house in the country, and I had never in all my life been out of London. No; nor had I ever seen a bit of green grass, except in the Drapers' Garden, which is near our house in Broad Street. Nor had I ever ridden in a railway carriage before that happy birthday.

I ran about the house, talking of where I was going, and rejoicing so that it was my birthday, that when I got into the train I was tired, and fell asleep.

When I awoke, I saw green fields on both sides of the train, and the fields were full, quite full, of bright, shining, yellow flowers, and the sheep and young lambs were feeding among them. The trees and hedges seemed to fly swiftly by us, and one field, and the sheep, and the lambs passed away. Then another field came, and that was full of cows. There was no end of these charming sights until we came to grandmamma's house, which stood all alone by itself, no house to be seen at all near it.

Grandmamma was very glad to see me. She first took me to the farmyard, and I peeped into the barn. There I saw a man thrashing, and as he beat the corn with his flail he made a great noise. Then I went to the pond where the ducks were swimming, and I saw the little wooden houses where the hens slept at night. The hens were feeding all over the yard, and the prettiest little chickens were feeding there too. Some little yellow ducklings had a hen for their mother. She was so frightened if they went near the water. Grandmamma says a hen is not esteemed a very wise bird.

We went out of the farmyard into the orchard. Oh, what a sweet place grandmamma's orchard is! There were pear-trees, and apple-trees, and peach-trees all in blossom. These blossoms were the prettiest flowers that ever were seen; and among the grass under the trees there grew buttercups, and cowslips, and daffodils, and blue-bells. I filled my lap with flowers, I filled my hair with flowers, and I carried as many flowers as I could in both my hands. But as I was going into the parlor to show them to mamma, I stumbled, and down I fell with all my treasures!

Next, there was a most wonderful garden to see, long and narrow, a straight gravel path down the middle of it, and at the end of the gravel walk there was a green arbor with a bench around it.

On one side of this garden there were a great many bee hives, and the bees sung as they worked. They had a beautiful flower-bed to gather their honey from, quite close to the hives.

After seeing the garden, I saw the cows milked, and that was the last sight I saw that day, for while I was telling mamma about the cows I fell fast asleep, and I suppose I was then put to bed.

The next morning my parents were gone. I cried sadly, but was comforted at hearing they would return in a month and fetch me home. Grandmamma gave me a little basket to gather my flowers in. I went out to the orchard, and before I had half filled my basket I forgot all my troubles.

The time I passed at my grandmamma's farm is always in my mind. Sometimes I think of the good-natured, pied cow that would let me stroke her while the dairy-maid was milking her. Then I fancy myself running after the dairy-maid into the nice, clean dairy, and see the pans full of milk and cream. Then I remember the wood-house; it had once been a barn, but being grown old, the wood was kept there. I used to peep about among the fagots to find the eggs the hens sometimes left there. A hen, grandmamma said, is a kindly bird, always laying more eggs than she wants on purpose to give them to her mistress for puddings and custards.

Nothing could have been more pleasant than the day the orchard was mowed. The hay smelled so sweet and I might toss it about as much as ever I pleased. It was green at first, and then turned yellow and dry, and was carried away in a cart to feed the horses.

When the currants and gooseberries were quite ripe, grandmamma had a sheep-shearing. All the sheep stood under the trees to be sheared. They were brought out of the field by old Spot, the shepherd dog. I stood at the gate and watched him drive them all in. When the shearers had cropped off all their wool, the sheep looked very clean, and white, and pretty. But, poor things, they ran shivering about with cold, so that it was a pity to see them.

Great preparations were being made all day for the sheep-shearing supper. Grandmamma said a sheep-shearing was not to be compared to a harvest-home, that was so much better. Then the oven was quite full of plum pudding, and the kitchen was very hot indeed with roasting beef; yet I can assure you that there was no want at all of either roast-beef or plum pudding at the sheep-shearing.

I was allowed to sit up until it was almost dark, to see the company at supper. They sat at a long oak table, which was finely carved, and as bright as a looking glass. After the happiest day, bed time will come. I sat up late, but at last grandmamma sent me to bed. Yet, though I went, I heard the company singing. The sound of their voices was very sweet indeed as they sang of the meadows and the sheep.

The common supper that we had every night was just as cheerful. Before the men came in out of the field, a large fagot was flung upon the fire. The wood used to crackle, and blaze, and smell delightfully. And then the crickets, who loved the fire, began to sing. The old shepherd loved the fire almost as well as the crickets did, and he would take his place in the chimney corner at supper time. He had a seat near the fireplace, quite under the chimney, and over his head the bacon hung.

When the shepherd was seated the milk was hung in a skillet over the fire, and then the men used to come and sit down at the long white table.

Sometimes, when I was at my grandmamma's farm house, I thought about London, how the houses stood close to each other, and what a noise the coaches made, and how many people there were in the streets. Then I usually went out into the old wood-house and played at being in London. I set up bits of wood for houses, and in one corner I made a little garden with grass and daisies, and that was the Draper's Garden.

I was sorry to have to go away from my grandmamma's farm before the harvesting but if I am allowed to return for it next year, I will tell you all about it.

THE PLOWMAN WHO FOUND CONTENT

A plowman paused in his work one day to rest. As he sat on the handle of his plow he fell thinking. The world had not been going well with him of late, and he could not help feeling downhearted. Just then he saw an old woman looking at him over the hedge.

"Good morning!" she said. "If you are wise you will take my advice."

"And what is your advice?" the plowman asked.

"Leave your plow and walk straight for two days. At the end of that time you will find yourself in the middle of a forest, and in front of you will be a tree towering high above the others. Cut it down and your fortune will be made."

With these words the old woman hobbled down the road, leaving the plowman wondering. He unharnessed his horses, drove them home, and said good-bye to his wife. Then, taking his axe, he started out.

At the end of two days he came to the tree, and set to work to cut it down. As it crashed to the ground a nest containing two eggs fell from its top-most branches. The shells of the eggs were broken, and out of one came a young eagle, while from the other rolled a small gold ring.

The eagle rapidly became larger, until it was of full size. Then, flapping its wings, it flew up.

"Thank you for my freedom," it called. "In token of my gratitude take this ring. It is a wishing ring. If you wish anything as you turn it around on your finger your wish will come true. But remember this, the ring contains only one wish, so think well before you use it."

The plowman put the ring on his finger and started home. Night was settling down as he entered the town. Almost the first person he sawwas a goldsmith standing at the door of his shop. So the plowman went up to him and asked him what the ring was worth.

"It is of no value," said the goldsmith.

The plowman laughed.

"Ah, Mr. Goldsmith," he said, "you have made a mistake. It is a wishing ring and will give me anything I care to wish for."

The goldsmith asked to see the ring again.

"Well, my good man," he said. "Never mind about the ring. I dare say you are far from home, and are in want of some supper and a bed for the night. Come in and spend the night with me."

So the plowman did this. But when he was sound asleep the goldsmith took the ring from his finger and put another, just like it, in its place.

Next morning the plowman set out with the false ring. The goldsmith closed the shutters of his shop and bolted the door. Then, turning the ring on his finger, he said, "I wish for a hundred thousand dollars."

Immediately there fell about him a shower of hard, bright silver. The dollars struck him on the head, the shoulders, the arms. They covered the floor. The floor gave way with their weight and the goldsmith, with his riches, fell into the cellar beneath.

Next morning, when the goldsmith did not open his shop as usual, the neighbors forced their way in and found him buried beneath the pile.

The plowman reached home and told his wife about the ring.

"Our fortune is made," he said, showing it to her. "Of course we must consider the matter well; then, when we have made up our minds as to what we need most, we can wish as I turn the ring on my finger."

"Suppose," said his wife, "we were to wish for a better farm? The land we have now is so small as to be almost useless."

"Yes," said the plowman. "But, if we work hard and spend little for a year or two, we might be able to buy as much as we want. Then we would still have our wish."

So it was agreed. For a year the plowman worked hard and his wife saved. Harvest time came and the crops were splendid. At the end of the year they were able to buy a nice farm, and still had some money left.

"There," said the man, "we have the land, and we still have our wish."

"Well," said his wife, "we could do very well with a horse and a cow."

"They are not worth wishing for," said he. "We can get them as we got the land."

So they went on working steadily and spending wisely for another year. At the end of that time they bought both the horse and the cow. It seemed great good fortune to them.

"We have all we wanted, and our wish left, also," they said.

So the years passed away. Every season saw the boundaries of the farm increase and the granaries grow fuller. All day long the farmer was about in the fields while his wife looked after the house and the dairy. Sometimes, as they sat alone of an evening, the plowman's wife would remind him of the unused ring and would talk of things she would like to have for the house. But he always said there was plenty of time.

The man and his wife grew old and gray. Then came a day when they both died, and the wishing ring had not been used. It was still on the plowman's finger as he had worn it for forty years. One of his sons was going to take it off, but the oldest said,

"Do not disturb it. There is some secret connected with it. Perhaps our mother gave it to him, for I have often seen her look longingly at it."

So the old plowman was buried with the ring which he had supposed to be a wishing ring. It was not, but it had brought more good fortune and happiness than all the wishing in the world could have given.

THE FARMER AND THE TROLL

There was once a man who owned a little farm, as fine and fruitful as you would care to see. He had always tended it himself, too, driving his own plow in the spring, and taking his two-wheeled cart to market in the fall with a load of apples, potatoes, and carrots.

All of a sudden, though, things began to go badly with the farmer. His milk curdled in the dairy and his horse kicked the traces on market day, spilling the load and laming herself into the bargain. The eggs were addled, and weeds choked and overran his garden, faster than he could pull them out.

"A troll is at the bottom of this," said the farmer's wife, and to prove it she led him to the dairy. There, on the white floor, were the prints in mud of tiny, tiny hob-nailed shoes. The same foot prints could be seen in the barn near the horse's stall, and that night the farmer saw a bright little light skipping about in the dusky garden. Of course he knew what that was, the one shining eye of a troll. So that was the cause of all his trouble. A troll had come to live on his farm.

Ordinarily a troll who selects a quiet place like a farm for his home is a peacefully inclined little man. He wants nothing but a bowl of porridge set out for him on the cellar steps once in a while, and a chance to creep in the house and curl up in a chimney corner of a cold evening, winking and blinking at the fire with his one eye. When a troll gets into mischief about a place, it is a sure sign that something has been done to displease him. So the farmer set out to try to find what he had done to vex the little man.

But look as high and as low as he could, he could find nothing, until one fine day in the spring he was plowing a nice little hill to plant a patch of potatoes. Suddenly his horse kicked the plow over, and the farmer heard a grumbling, growling little voice coming up through the earth.

"There you go again," said the voice, "tearing up my roof just as you did a year ago in the spring. Don't you know that this is my hill, and that I live down here under it?" It was the troll that spoke.

Well, the farmer was much put out to know that he had plowed up the roof of the troll's house and he did not know what to do about it, for it was his hill, also, and a fine, sunny slope for raising a crop. At last, though, he thought of a plan and he called down through the hill to the troll.

"Well, now, little master, I am sorry indeed to have disturbed you so and I am ready to make any recompense that I can. What do you say to this? I will plow, sow, and reap the hill each year, doing every bit of the work myself, mind you, and we will have the crops, turn and turn about. One year you shall have everything that grows above the ground and I will take only what grows below the ground; the next year you shall have what lies below, while my share will be what grows above. That is a fair bargain, is it not?"

"Very good," said the troll. "I am perfectly well satisfied. And this year I would like whatever grows above the ground."

The farmer chuckled to himself. That satisfied him, too, for he was planting potatoes. But when they had sprouted and grown, up through the hill came the troll with a little scythe over his shoulder and cut all the potato tops, taking them home with him. A fine harvest he thought he had gathered.

The next season it was the troll's turn to have what grew below ground, so the farmer sowed the hill with corn. When the corn was ripe the troll did not appear at all. He was down under the hill busily cutting the roots of the corn, well content with this share of the harvest. So the farmer was crafty in his planting. The next season it was carrots, and the next, beans. The troll gathered his carrot tops and his bean roots, and laid them away carefully for the winter.

Which goes to show how easily you can satisfy a troll, but what a poor farmer he is.

SCHOOL

A PURITAN SCHOOL-DAY

Peregrine fastened his long black cloak, and Patience smoothed her white apron and tied the strings of her close-fitting bonnet beneath her dimpled chin. The brother and sister crossed the threshold of the log house which was their home in old Plymouth, almost three hundred years ago, and started to walk across the corn fields and through a patch of woodland, lying between their house and the next cabin.

They were two little Puritan children, going to school.

They laughed and pointed happily to the full ears of corn as they crossed the fields. There would be a good harvest, they knew, and that meant plenty of hot corn-meal mush filling the big copper kettle that hung over their fireplace, and corn would fill the huge brick oven. But as Peregrine and Patience crept softly between the great pine trees of the wood, they clasped each other's hands more tightly, and started to see a red-winged bird dart out of the branches. "Suppose it had been the bright feather head-dress of an Indian," they whispered. One was very apt to meet Indians on the way to school in those old-time days.

The long distance was travelled in safety, though. Promptly at eight o'clock, the two little Puritans knocked at the door of a second log house and it was opened by their neighbor, Mistress Endicott. There was no school-bell, there were no desks and comfortable chairs and blackboards and picture books. Mistress Endicott had risen from her spinning wheel, that stood by the fireplace, to let in Peregrine and Patience, and a dozen other small boys and girls of Plymouth. There was no real schoolhouse as yet in Plymouth. Mistress Endicott kept house, and tended her garden, and taught all the children of the neighborhood as well.

There were long settles beside the fireplace and here the children seated themselves, Peregrine on one side, and Patience on the other, to study their lessons. They were given queer little books, called the New England Primer, in wooden covers, and having funny, tiny pictures for each letter of the alphabet, and beside each, a jingle. There were verses to be learned from the Bible, too. Patience held her primer up close to her nose and studied very diligently, but Peregrine's eyes wandered out of the window and toward the blue sky. He was thinking of a kite he planned to make when school was over.

"Class stand, and recite," Mistress Endicott said suddenly, stopping the whir of her spinning wheel only a moment to call the children, for industry and learning had to go on at the same time in those old days in the Colonies.

At once the boys and girls rose and stood in front of their teacher, the copper toes of their stout shoes placed exactly on a long crack in the bare floor. Then they read aloud, while Mistress Endicott's wheel whirred on. It sounded as if a hive of bees were humming in the schoolroom, but the good dame could listen and spin at the same time. She knew very well if a child made a mistake.

Across the room there were some long benches made of logs, split in two, and with other logs to support them. When the class had finished reading, they took their places at these benches, the boys to do sums, and the girls to work on their samplers. Each little Puritan girl had brought her sewing bag to school, and was working her name, the date of her birthday, and a verse of some kind on a square of canvas, which made her sampler. Patience was working a very fine sampler indeed. Her mother had given her some bright crewels thatshe had brought from England, and Patience was using them to embroider a basket of flowers in cross-stitch in one corner of her sampler. Patience bent low over her sewing, until her long flaxen braids almost touched the floor. At last, though, she looked up.

Where was Peregrine, she wondered? He was not on the bench with the other boys. At last Patience saw her brother. Oh, dear, how disgraced she felt! Peregrine had not learned his lesson well, because he had looked out of the window. He had not recited well, so Mistress Endicott had put the dunce's cap on his head and he stood in a corner where all could see him.

But Peregrine's punishment did not last for long. He was soon forgiven and busy bringing in logs of wood to pile on the fire. Already the days had a touch of frost in them, and Peregrine's father had sent the school-mistress a load of wood. This was to pay her for teaching Patience and Peregrine. The other children's parents paid her in corn, and barley, and other good things that they raised on their farms. If the teacher had been a man, the Puritan mothers would have spun and woven some warm cloth to make him a coat, or knitted him a woollen muffler, or a pair of stockings.

Late in the afternoon, after their luncheon of cold hasty pudding and apples and more study and reading, school was over. Peregrine and Patience each made a low bow before Mistress Endicott, went out of the door, and started home. The dusk was already falling, but they ran, and sang as they hurried along to keep up their courage.

There, at last, was the twinkle of the tallow candle which their mother had set in the window to lead them home. She was waiting for them at the door, and the kettle was singing on the hob. The school-day, almost three hundred years ago, was over.

THE LAST CLASS

That morning, Franz was taking his way very slowly to school. He had a great dread of being scolded, particularly as the school-master had said that the lesson for the day would be on participles about which Franz did not know a word. Suddenly an idea came to him. He would go through the fields.

It was so warm, so clear. He heard the blackbirds whistling on the borders of the wood, and in the meadow, behind the saw-mill, the Prussians were drilling. Then, as he passed on by the residence of the mayor, Franz saw them putting a notice on the gate. There, for two years, had been given out all the bad news; lost battles for Alsace, calls to arms, the orders of the command. The blacksmith and his apprentice were putting up the notice, and Franz called,

"What has happened, that they are posting a bulletin again?" But the blacksmith spoke gruffly,

"Why do you loiter, little one? It is not safe. Run along quickly to school."

So Franz made haste at last, although he was sure that the blacksmith was not in earnest, and he arrived all breathless, at his class.

School seemed, somehow, very different to Franz that morning. There was ordinarily a good deal of noise as the children came in from the street, desks were opened, and lessons were repeated out loud and all in unison, and the school-master pounded with his ruler on his table.

Now, however, there was silence.

Although Franz was late, the school-master looked at him without the least anger, and spoke softly as he said, "Go quickly to your place, my little Franz. We have already begun without you."

Franz seated himself at his desk. Only then, his fear gone, he noticed that the master had on his best green frock coat, his finely plaited shirt and the black silk cap that he never wore except on a day when there were prizes given out in school. All the children were extraordinarily quiet. But what surprised Franz the most was to see at the back of the room, seated on the benches which were ordinarily empty, the people of the village. There was an old soldier with his tri-colored flag, the old mayor of the town, the postman, and many others. Everyone seemed sad. And the old soldier had a spelling book, ragged on the edges, that he held open on his knees, as he followed the pages through his great spectacles.

As little Franz watched all this, astonished, the school-master rose from his chair, and in the same grave, soft voice in which he had spoken to the boy, he said,

"My children, this is the last time that I shall teach your class. The order has come from Berlin that no language but German shall be taught in the schools of Alsace and Lorraine. Your new master arrives to-morrow. To-day, you will have your last lesson in French. I pray that you will be very attentive."

Franz's last lesson in French! And he could not write it without mistakes! He remembered all the time that he had wasted, the lessons he had missed in hunting for birds' nests, or skating on the river. He thought of his books that would remind him always now, of his laziness—his grammar, his history, a present from his friend, the school-master, from whom he must part now with so much pain. In the midst of these thoughts, Franz heard his name called. It was his turn to recite.

He would have given a great deal to be able to recite the famous order of the participles, without a mistake, to give them clearly, and without a fault. But he confused them at the first word, and remained standing beside his desk, his heart trembling, not daring to raise his head. He heard the school-master speaking to him,

"I am not going to rebuke you, little Franz. You are already punished. Every day you have said to yourself, 'Bah, I have plenty of time; to-morrow I will study.'"

"Ah, that has been the great fault in our Alsace, that of always putting off learning until another day. In the meantime, all the world has been quite right in saying of us, 'How is it that you pretend to be French, and yet are not able to read and write your own language!' Of all who are here, my poor little Franz, you are not the only one at fault. We all must reproach ourselves."

Then the school-master told them of his longing to still teach the children the French language. He said that it would always be the most beautiful language of the world. He said that he wanted it treasured in Alsace and never forgotten, because, when a people fall into slavery it is almost like holding the key to their prison if they can speak to each other in the same tongue. Afterward he took a grammar and went over the lesson with the children. All that he read seemed suddenly quite easy to Franz; he had never attended so well, and never before had he understood how patient the school-master was in his explanations.

When the lesson was finished, writing was begun. For this last day, the master had prepared fresh copies.

France, Alsace. France, Alsace.

The copies were like little flags, floating all over the schoolroom from the tops of the desks. Nothing broke the great silence but the scratching of the pens upon the paper. Suddenly some May bugs flew in through the window, but no one noticed them. On the roof of the school some pigeons began to coo, and Franz thought to himself, "Will it be commanded that the birds, too, speak to us in a foreign language?"

From time to time, as Franz lifted his eyes from his paper, he saw the school-master sitting quietly in his chair, and looking all about him, as if he wanted to remember always every child and every bit of furniture in his little schoolroom. Only think, for forty years, he had been there in his place, with the playground facing him, and his class always as full! Only the benches and the desks which had once been polished were worn from usage now; the walnut trees in the yard had grown very large, and the hop vine that he, himself, had planted twined now above the window and as far as the roof. It was breaking the heart of the school-master to leave all these things.

But he had the courage to carry on the class to the very end. After the writing lesson, he began the lesson in history. Afterward, the little ones sang their A. B. C.'s all together and at the end of the room the old soldier took off his spectacles and, holding his spelling book in his two hands, he read off the letters with them.

Suddenly the clock in the tower of the village church sounded the hour of noon. Instantly, the trumpet call of the Prussians, returning from their drilling, burst through the windows. The school-master rose, quite pale, in his place. Never had he seemed so great to the children.

"My friends," he said, "my little friends, I—"

But he could say no more; he was not able to speak the words. He turned to the blackboard and, taking a piece of chalk, he wrote upon it,

"Vive la France!"

Afterward, he remained there, his head resting against the wall, and, without speaking, he made a sign with his hand.

"It is finished. You are dismissed."

TIMOTHY'S SHOES

The godmother arrived for the christening, dressed in plum-colored satin and carrying a small brown parcel.

"Fortunatus' purse!" whispered one of the guests, nudging his neighbor.

"A mere trifle for the boy," said the fairy godmother, laying the parcel down on the table. "It is a very common gift to come from my hands, but I trust it will prove useful."

She untied the string of the parcel and gave the baby's mother—what do you think?

A small pair of strong leather shoes, copper-tipped and heeled!

"They'll never wear out, my dear," she said. "And, after all, my little gift is not quite so shabby as it looks. These shoes, have another quality besides that of not wearing out. The little feet that are in them cannot very easily go wrong."

"Mrs. Godmother's broomstick is at the door," shouted some one. So the fairy godmother took her departure.

As years went by and her family increased, the mother learned the full value of the fairy shoes. Her nine boys wore them in turn, but they never wore them out. So long as these shoes were on their feet, they were pretty sure to go where they were sent and to come back when they were wanted. So, at last, the fairy shoes descended to the ninth and youngest boy, and became Timothy's.

Now the eighth boy had very small feet and had worn the shoes rather longer than the others, and Timothy got them somewhat later than usual. Even though she was very conscientious, Timothy's mother found it hard not to spoil the youngest in the family. Master Timothy was wilful, and his feet became used to taking their own way before he stepped into the fairy shoes. He played truant from school, and was late for dinner so often that at length his mother decided that something must be done about Timothy. One morning the leather of the fairy shoes was brightly blacked and the copper tips polished, and Timothy wore them for the first time.

"Now, Timothy, dear, I know you will be a good boy," his mother said. "And mind you don't loiter or play truant, for if you do, these shoes will pinch you horribly, and you'll be sure to be found out."

Timothy looked as if he didn't believe it. He was off like an arrow from a bow, and he gave not one more thought to what his mother had said.

The winter had been very cold, the spring had been fitful and stormy, but May had suddenly burst upon the country with one broad, bright smile of sunshine and flowers. If Timothy had loitered on the way to school when the frost nipped his nose, and the ground was muddy, and the March winds crept up his jacket sleeves, it was hard to hurry now when every nook had a flower and every bush a bird.

It was wrong to play truant, but still it was very tempting. Twir-r-r-r, up to the sky flew the larks. Down in the marsh below the king-cups blossomed, as shining as gold.

Once or twice Timothy stopped, but his shoes pinched him and he ran on all the more willingly because a bright butterfly went before him. But where the path ran on above the marsh, and he looked down and saw the king-cups, he dismissed all thoughts of school. The bank was long and steep, but that did not matter to him. King-cups he must have; no other flowers would do. He threw his school bag on the grass, and began to scramble down the bank.

Timothy turned his feet toward the king-cups, but his shoes seemed resolved to go to school. As he persisted in going toward the marsh, he had such twitches and twinges as the fairy shoes pinched him that it seemed as if his feet would be wrenched off. But Timothy was a resolute little fellow, and he managed to drag himself, shoes and all, down to the marsh.

Then he could not find a king-cup within reach. Not one grew on the safe edge, but, like so many Will-o'-the-wisps, they shone out of the depths of the treacherous bogs. Timothy wandered round the marsh; pinch, jerk, every step hurt more than the one before. At last, desperate with pain and disappointment, he fairly jumped into a patch of the flowers that looked fairly near, and was at once ankle deep in water. But, to Timothy's delight, the wet mud soaked the shoes off his feet, and he was able to wade about among the rushes, reeds, and king-cups, happy.

And he was none the worse, although he ought to have been. He moved about very cautiously, feeling his way with a stick from tussock to tussock of reedy grass, wondering why his eight brothers had never thought of taking off the fairy shoes when they grew troublesome.

At last, though, Timothy began to feel tired. He hurt his foot on a sharp stump. A fat green frog jumped up in his face and so startled him that he nearly fell backwards in the water. He had gathered more king-cups than he could hold. So he scrambled out of the marsh, climbed up the bank, cleaned himself as well as he could, and thought he would go on to school.

Now, with all his faults, Timothy was not a coward or a liar. With a quaking heart he made up his mind to tell the teacher that he had played truant. He was trying to make up his mind just exactly what he would say first and had got no farther than, "Please, ma'am —" when he found himself in the schoolroom, and under the teacher's very eye. Timothy did not see her frown; he did not hear the children's titters. His eyes were fixed upon the schoolroom floor, where — beside Timothy's desk — stood the fairy shoes, very muddy, and with a yellow king-cup sticking up out of each.

"You've been in the marsh, Timothy," said his teacher. "Put on your shoes."

So Timothy put them on, and when his lessons were over, he let his shoes take him straight home.

FALL

THE THREE APPLES

The old apple tree stood in the orchard with the other trees, and all summer long it had stretched out its branches wide to catch the rain and the sun to make its apples grow round and ripe. Now it was fall, and on the old apple tree were three great apples as yellow as gold and larger than any other apples in the whole orchard. The apple tree stretched and reached as far as it could, until the branch on which the three gold apples grew hung over the orchard wall. There were the three great apples, waiting for some one to pick them, and as the wind blew through the leaves of the apple tree it seemed to sing:

"Here in the orchard are apples three,Who uses one well shall a treasure see."

And one morning Gerald came down the lane that passed by the orchard wall. He looked longingly at the three gold apples, wishing, wishing that he might have one. Just then the wind sang its song again in the leaves of the apple tree and, plump, down to the ground, right at Gerald's feet, fell one of the three gold apples.

He picked it up and turned it round and round in his hands. How sweet it smelled, and how mellow and juicy it was! Gerald could think of nothing so good to do with such a beautiful ripe apple as to eat it. He put it to his mouth and took a great bite of it, then another bite, and another. Soon there was nothing left of the apple but the core, which Gerald threw away. He smacked his lips and went on his way, but the wind in the apple trees sang, sorrowfully, after him:

"Here in the orchard are apples two,But gone is the treasure that fell for you."

And after a while Hilda came down the lane that passed by the orchard wall. She looked up at the two beautiful gold apples that hung on the branch of the old apple tree, and she listened to the wind as it sang in the branches to her:

"Here in the orchard are apples two,A treasure they hold for a child like you."

Then the wind blew harder and, plump, an apple fell in the lane right in front of Hilda.

She picked it up joyfully. She had never seen so large and so golden an apple. She held it carefully in her clasped hands and thought what a pity it would be to eat it, because then it would be gone.

"I will keep this gold apple always," Hilda said, and she wrapped it up in the clean handkerchief that was in her pocket. Then Hilda went home, and there she laid away in a drawer the gold apple that the old apple tree had given her, closing the drawer tightly. The apple lay inside, in the dark, and all wrapped up, for many days, until it spoiled. And when Hilda next went down the lane and past the orchard, the wind in the apple tree sang to her:

"Only one apple where once there were two,Gone is the treasure I gave to you."

Last of all, Rudolph went down the lane one fine fall morning when the sun was shining warm and the wind was out. There, hanging over the orchard wall, he saw just one great gold apple that seemed to him the most beautiful apple that he had ever seen. As he stood looking up at it, the wind in the apple tree sang to him, and it said:

"Round and gold on the apple tree,A wonderful treasure, hanging, see!"

Then the wind blew harder, and down fell the last gold apple of the three into Rudolph's waiting hands.

He held it a long time and looked at it as Gerald and Hilda had, thinking how good it would be to eat, and how pretty it would be to look at if he were to save it. Then he decided not to do either of these things. He took his jack-knife out of his pocket and cut the gold apple in half, straight across, and exactly in the middle between the blossom and the stem.

Oh, the surprise that waited for Rudolph inside the apple! There was a star, and in each point of the star lay a small black seed. Rudolph carefully took out all the seeds and climbed over the orchard wall, holding them in his hand. The earth in the orchard was still soft, for the frost had not yet come. Rudolph made holes in the earth and in each hole he dropped an apple seed. Then he covered up the seeds and climbed back over the wall to eat his apple, and then go on his way.

But as Rudolph walked down the lane, the orchard wind followed him, singing to him from every tree and bush,

"A planted seed is a treasure won.The work of the apple is now well done."

THE HORN OF PLENTY

Deïanira was one of the most beautiful of princesses who lived in the long ago times of the Greek gods and goddesses. It seemed as if all the loveliness of the world in this, its story time, was hers. Her hair was bright with the yellow of the first spring sunshine, and her eyes were as blue as the skies of spring. Summer had touched Deïanira's cheeks with the pink of rose petals, and the colors of the autumn fruits shone in her jewels, crimson, and purple, and gold. Her robes were as white and sparkling as the snows of winter, and all the music of soft winds, and bird songs, and rippling brooks was in this princess' voice.

Because of her beauty, and her goodness which even surpassed it, princes came from all over the earth to ask Deïanira's father, Æneus, if she might go home to their kingdoms and be their queen. But to all these Æneus replied that to none but the strongest would he give the princess.

There were many tests of these strangers' skill and strength in games and wrestling, but one by one they failed. At last there were only two left, Hercules, who could hold the sky on his great shoulders, and Acheloüs, the river-god, who could twist and twine through the fields and make them fertile. Each thought himself the greater of the two, and it lay between them which should gain the princess, by his prowess, to be his queen.

Hercules was great of limb, and of powerful strength. Beneath his shaggy eyebrows, his eyes gleamed like coals of fire. His garment was of lion skins, and his staff was a young tree. But Acheloüs was able to slip between the huge fingers of Hercules. He was as slim and graceful as a willow tree, and dressed in the green of foliage. He wore a crown of water lilies on his fair hair, and carried a staff made of twined reeds. When Acheloüs spoke, his voice was like the rippling of a stream.

"The princess Deïanira shall be mine!" said Acheloüs. "I will make her the queen of the river lands. The music of the waters shall be always in her ears, and the plenty that follows wherever I flow shall make her rich."

"No," shouted Hercules. "I am the strength of the earth. Deïanira is mine. You shall not have her."

Then the river-god grew very angry. His green robe changed to the black of the sea in a storm, and his voice was as loud as a mountain cataract. Acheloüs could be almost as powerful as Hercules when he was angered.

"How do you dare claim this royal maiden?" he roared, "you, who have mortal blood in your veins? I am a god, and the king of the waters. Wherever I take my way through the earth, grains and fruits ripen, and flowers bud and bloom. The princess is mine by right."

Hercules frowned as he advanced toward the river-god. "Your strength is only in words," he said scornfully. "My strength is in my arm. If you would win Deïanira, it must be by hand-to-hand combat." So the river-god threw off his garments and Hercules his lions' skins, and the two fought for the hand of the princess.

It was a brave and valorous battle. Neither yielded; both stood firm. Acheloüs slipped in and out of Hercules' mighty grasp a dozen times, but at last Hercules' greater strength overpowered him. Hercules held the river-god fast by his neck, panting for breath. But Acheloüs knew magic arts which he could practise. He suddenly changed himself into a long, slippery serpent. He twisted out of Hercules' grasp, and darted out his forked tongue at him, showing his poisonous fangs.

Hercules was not yet outdone, though. He laughed in scorn at the serpent. While he was still in his cradle, Hercules had strangled two serpents, and he had met a Hydra with a hundred heads that he had cut off. He was not in the least afraid of the river-god in the form of a serpent, but gripped the creature by the back of its neck, ready to strangle it.

Acheloüs struggled in vain to escape, and at last tried his magic arts again. In a second the serpent had changed its form to that of a bellowing ferocious bull. With its horns lowered, it charged upon Hercules.

But Hercules was still unvanquished. He seized hold of the bull's horns, bent its head, grasped its brawny neck, and throwing it down buried the horns in the ground. Then he broke off one of the horns with his iron strong hand, and held it up in the air, shouting,

"Victory! The princess is mine!"

Acheloüs returned to his own shape, and, crying with pain, ran from the castle grounds where the combat had taken place, and did not stop until he had plunged into a cooling stream.

It had been right that Hercules should triumph, for his was strength of arm, not that of trickery. Deïanira stood by his side, and the goddess of plenty came forward to give the conqueror his reward.

She took the great horn which Hercules had torn from Acheloüs' head and heaped it high with the year's stores. Ripe grain, grapes, apples, plums, nuts, pomegranates, figs, and all the other fruits of the autumn filled the horn, and overflowed it. The wood-nymphs and the water-nymphs came and twined the horn with vines, and crimson leaves, and the last bright flowers of the year. Then they carried this horn of plenty, high above their heads, and gave it to Hercules, and his beautiful queen, Deïanira. It was the richest gift the gods could make, the year's harvest.

And ever since that long-ago story time of the Greeks the horn of plenty has stood for the year's blessing of us; it is full to overflowing with the fruits of the harvest.

THE GOOSE WHO TRIED TO KEEP THE SUMMER

There was once an old Wild Goose who had led the flock of other wild geese every fall for years and years on their way south. He had a thick coat of white feathers, he wore orange-colored boots, and his bill was like a gold trumpet when he opened it to call,

Honk, honk, honk!

That was the signal for the others to rise from the meadows and the marshes. He flew at their head, and the rest followed, one line on one side and one line on the other. He thought himself most important.

Over the woods and the fields and the waters, every one looked for the old Wild Goose in the fall.

Honk, honk, honk!

That was the Wild Goose telling them that it was time to get ready for the winter in the woods, and in the fields, and over the waters. He knew they waited for him, so he had grown to feel very proud of himself. He lived in a marsh that was sheltered on both sides by trees and was comfortable, even if there was a frost now and then. A robin had once stayed in those trees all winter and he sang proudly about it.

"Why do I trouble to go south?" the old Wild Goose thought to himself. "The weather here will not grow cold if I stay. Honk, honk; I shall not trouble myself to migrate this fall and then we shall see what will happen! Very likely I shall keep the summer!"

No one knew what the Goose had decided, and they listened for him.

The dandelion looked up from her home in the field and bobbed her little head as she waited to hear the call of the Wild Goose. Every fall she had sent a flock of winged seeds flying along with him as far as they could go. Then they would drop in other fields and begin making more dandelions for next year. She knew she must not wait too long. She listened, but she did not hear his honk, honk, honk!

Puff, whirr; off she sent her tiny winged seed without the call of the old Wild Goose.

The farmer buttoned his coat tightly and looked up among the gray clouds to see the Goose. Every fall he listened to hear the call of the Wild Goose as he gathered his harvest. He knew, though, that he must not wait too long. He took his grain to the mill and filled his barn with red apples, and orange pumpkins, and yellow corn. He made warmer beds for the cows and horses, and cut logs to burn in his fireplace. He was soon ready for winter without the help of the old Wild Goose.

The brook called and called for the Goose. Every fall she waited for him to fly over and then she built her winter roof, for she knew then that no other wild bird would need to drink from her waters. She must not wait long, though. There were her fish, and the water spider, and the beaver to shelter all winter. So the brook forgot, at last, about the old Wild Goose and built a smooth ice roof to keep her children warm until spring.

Honk, honk, cried all the other wild geese. "It is time to migrate! Come with us!"

Honk, honk, honk, cried the old Wild Goose, from the sheltered marsh where he did not know what was going on. "I am not flying south this year. I am staying north to keep the summer."

Honk, honk, "What a terrible time it will be!" cried all the other geese. They talked among themselves, saying that no good could come of turning the seasons about, and of how he would probably be eaten in the end. Then they selected a wise young goose who had been end man the year before, and they made him their leader. His boots were quite as orange and his bill as golden as those of the old Goose, and he could honk very well indeed. They went south with the new leader.

Soon Winter came. He wore a crown of snowflakes. His cloak was embroidered with frost, and he carried a huge icicle as his sceptre. Every one was ready for him. The dandelion bowed her bare head as Winter passed. The barn doors were closed, and the cattle stood, safe and warm, in their stalls.

But the Wild Goose felt Winter coming. An icy wind blew through his feathers. His throat was so stiff with cold that he could not blow his trumpet. His orange boots froze stiff as the marsh turned to ice.

"It must be the winter coming in spite of me," he thought to himself. "It seems that I have not kept him away after all. I shall die, for he will freeze me. What shall I do?"

Then a sunbeam, that was still strong enough to help a little, heard the faint cries of the old Wild Goose and was sorry for him. She melted the ice so that the Goose could pull out his feet, first one, and then the other. She stood for a moment in Winter's path as the Goose rose and stretched his stiff wings, and then started south.

The chilly air was like a blast on his head. He was obliged to fly slowly, but he managed to call as he went,

"Honk, honk, Here I am. I fly to tell you that Winter is coming."

He looked down at the woods, and the fields, and the waters. How strange! They had known it. They had not waited for the call of the old Wild Goose.

THANKSGIVING
CHIP'S THANKSGIVING

They had got "way through," as Terry said, to the nuts. It had been a beautiful Thanksgiving dinner so far. Grandmother's sweet face beamed down the length of the great table, over all the little curly grand-heads, at Grandfather's face. Everybody felt very thankful.

"I wish all the children this side of the North Pole had some turkey, too, and squash, and cranberry — and things," Silence said quietly. Silence was always thinking of beautiful things like that.

"And some nuts," Terry said, setting his small white teeth into the meat of a big fat walnut. "It wouldn't seem like Thanksgiving without nuts."

"I know somebody who would be thankful with just nuts," smiled Grandfather. "Indeed, I think that he would rather have them for all the courses of his Thanksgiving dinner!"

"Just nuts! No turkey, or pudding, or anything?" The curly grand-heads all bobbed up from their plates and nut pickers in amazement. Just nuts!

"Yes! Guess who he is." Grandfather's laughing eyes twinkled up the long table at Grandmother. "I'll give you three guesses apiece, beginning with Heart's Delight. Guess number one, Heart's Delight."

"Chip." Heart's Delight had guessed it at the very first guess.

"Chip!" laughed all the little grand-boys and girls. "Why, of course! Chip! He would rather have just nuts for his Thanksgiving dinner."

"I wish he had some of mine," cried Silence.

"And mine!" cried Terry, and all the others wished that he had some of theirs. What a Thanksgiving dinner little Chip would have had!

"He's got plenty, thank you." It was the shy little voice of Heart's Delight. A soft pink color had come into her round cheeks. Everybody looked at her in surprise, for how did Heart's Delight know that Chip had plenty of nuts? Then Terry remembered something.

"Oh, that's where her nuts went to!" he cried. "Heart's Delight gave them to Chip! We couldn't think what she had done with them all."

Heart's Delight's cheeks grew pinker—very pink indeed.

"Yes, that's where," said Silence, leaning over to squeeze one of Heart's Delight's little hands. And sure enough, it was. In the beautiful nut month of October, when the children went after their winter's supply of nuts, Heart's Delight had left all her little rounded heap just where bright-eyed, nut-hungry Squirrel Chip would be sure to find them and hurry them away to his hole. And Chip had found them, she was sure, for not one was left when she went back to see the next day.

"Why, maybe, this very minute—right now—Chip is cracking his Thanksgiving dinner," Terry laughed.

"Just as we are! Maybe he's come to the nut course—but they are all nut courses. And maybe he's sitting up at his table with the rest of his folks, thanksgiving to Heart's Delight," Silence said.

Heart's Delight's little shy face nearly hid itself over her plate. This was dreadful! It was necessary to change the conversation at once, and a dear little thought came to her aid.

"But I'm afraid Chip hasn't got any grandfather or grandmother at his Thanksgiving," she said softly. "I should think it would be hard to give thanks without any grandfather and grandmother."

THE FIRST THANKSGIVING

All through the first summer and the early part of autumn the Pilgrims were busy and happy. They had planted and cared for their first fields of corn. They had found wild strawberries in the meadows, raspberries on the hillsides, and wild grapes in the woods.

In the forest just back of the village wild turkeys and deer were easily shot. In the shallow waters of the bay there was plenty of fish, clams, and lobsters.

The summer had been warm, with a good deal of rain and much sunshine; and so, when autumn came, there was a fine crop of corn.

"Let us gather the fruits of our first harvest and rejoice together," said Governor Bradford.

"Yes," said Elder Brewster, "let us take a day upon which we may thank God for all our blessings and invite to it our Indian friends who have been so kind to us."

The Pilgrims said that one day was not enough; so they planned to have a celebration for a whole week.

The great Indian chief, Massasoit, came with ninety of his bravest warriors, all gaily dressed in deerskins, feathers, and fox tails, with their faces smeared with red, white, and yellow paint. As a sign of rank, Massasoit wore a string of bones and a bag of tobacco around his neck. In his belt he carried a long knife. His face was painted red, and his hair was daubed with oil.

There were only eleven buildings in the whole of Plymouth village, four log storehouses, and seven little log dwelling-houses, so the Indian guests ate and slept out of doors. This did not matter for it was one of those warm weeks in the season that we call Indian summer.

To supply meat for the occasion four men had already been sent out to hunt wild turkeys. They killed enough in one day to last the company almost a week.

Massasoit helped the feast along by sending some of his best hunters into the woods. They brought back five deer which they gave to their pale face friends, that all might have enough to eat.

Under the trees were built long, rude tables on which were piled baked clams, broiled fish, roasted turkey, and venison. The young Pilgrim women helped serve the food to the hungry redskins. We shall always remember two of the fair young girls who waited on the first Thanksgiving table. One was Mary Chilton, who leaped first from the boat at Plymouth Rock. The other was Mary Allerton. She lived for seventy-eight years after this first Thanksgiving; of those who came over in the Mayflower she was the last to die.

What a merry time everybody had during that week! How the mothers must have laughed as they told about the first Monday morning on Cape Cod, when they all went ashore to wash their clothes! It must have been a big washing, for there had been no chance to do it at sea, so stormy had been the long voyage of sixty-three days. They little thought that Monday would always after be kept as washing day. One proud Pilgrim mother, we may be sure, showed her baby boy, Peregrine White.

And so the fun went on. In the daytime the young men ran races, played games, and had a shooting match. Every night the Indians sang and danced for their friends; and to make the party still more lively they gave every now and then a shrill war whoop that made the woods echo in the still night air.

The third day came. Massasoit had been well treated, and would have liked to stay longer, but he said that he could not be away from his camp for more than three days. So the pipe of peace was silently passed around. Then, taking their gifts of glass beads and trinkets, the Indian King and his warriors said farewell to their English friends and began their long march through the woods to their wigwams on Mount Hope Bay.

On the last day of this Thanksgiving party, Elder Brewster preached the first Thanksgiving sermon and all the Pilgrims united in thanking God for His goodness to them.

The first Thanksgiving was nearly three hundred years ago. Since that time, Thanksgiving has been kept by the people of our nation as the great family festival of the year. At this time children and grandchildren return to the old home, the long table is spread, and brothers and sisters, who had been separated, again seat themselves side by side.

Thanksgiving is our season of sweet and blessed memories.

THE KING'S THANKSGIVING

Every child in the village was very much excited on account of the news that had come down from the castle on the hill.

Because it had been such a rich harvest, the fields yellow with grain and the orchards crimson with fruit, the King was going to keep a thanksgiving day. He was going to ask some child from the village to come up the hill to the castle and eat dinner with the Prince and Princess. It was rumored, too, that this child would be given good gifts by the King. But it must be a very special kind of child indeed. That they all knew.

Then the village children remembered everything that had been told them by their mothers, and their grandmothers, and their great-grandmothers about the castle kitchen. Scores of cooks and scullery boys were kept busy there night and day. The fires always glowed to roast the rich fowls that turned on the spits. The cake bowls and the soup pots were never empty. Spices and herbs from far countries, strawberries when the ground was covered with snow, ices of all the rainbow colors, and cream so thick that a knife could cut it—all these were to be found in the King's kitchen.

There were dishes of gold and silver upon which to serve the fine foods, and a hothouse of rare flowers with which to deck the table, and linen as fine as a cobweb and as beautiful in pattern as snowflakes to cover it. Oh, a thanksgiving day in the castle would be very wonderful indeed, the children thought, and each hoped that he or she would be chosen to go.

The day before this day of thanksgiving the messenger of the King came down from the castle and went from door to door of the homes in the village. He went first to the house of the burgomaster. It was a very pretentious house with tall pillars in front, and it stood on a wide street. It seemed likely that the burgomaster's child might be chosen to go with the messenger to the castle for the thanksgiving. She was dressed in silk, and her hair was curled, and the burgomaster had packed a great hamper with sweets as an offering for the King.

"Are you ready to keep the feast as the King would like you to?" asked the messenger.

"Oh, yes!" said the burgomaster's child. "I have on my best dress, and here are plenty of sweets to eat. Will you take me?"

But the messenger shook his head, for the child was not ready.

Then the King's messenger went on until he came to the house where the captain of the guards lived. The captain's little boy was quite sure that he would be chosen to go with the messenger to the castle for the thanksgiving. He wore a uniform with silver braid and buttons like that which the guards wore. A sword hung at his side, and he wore a soldier's cap. He held the cap in his hand, so that he could put it on quickly.

"Are you ready to keep the thanksgiving day as the King would like you to?" asked the messenger.

"Oh, yes!" said the child of the captain of the guards. "I have my sword here and I can fight any one who crosses our path on the way to the castle. Will you take me?"

But the messenger went on again and he came to the baker's shop. The baker's boy stood at the door, dressed in his best white suit, and holding an empty basket on his arm. He was quite sure that he would be chosen to go to the palace, for his father's bake shop was an important place in the village. They measured their flour carefully, and weighed the loaves so that they might receive the utmost penny for each. They very seldom had any crumbs left for the poor, but they were selling a great deal of bread every day.

"Are you ready to keep the thanksgiving day as the King would like you to?" the messenger asked of the baker's boy.

"Oh, yes!" the boy said. "I have this basket to gather up whatever remains of the King's feast and bring it home with me. The King would not want anything wasted. Will you take me?"

But the messenger shook his head a third time, for the child was not ready.

Then he did not know which way to go, and he began to think that he would not be able to find any guest for the King's feast. As he waited, he saw two children, a girl and a boy, coming toward him. They were poor children, and one was leading the other, for he was lame. The messenger looked at them. The little girl had eyes like stars and her hair, blowing in the November wind, was like a cloud made golden by the sunset. She held her head so high, and smiled so bravely that no one would have noticed her old dress and the holes in her coat. The messenger stood in the road in front of her and spoke to her.

"Are you ready to keep the thanksgiving day as the King would like you to?" he asked.

The little girl looked up in the messenger's face in surprise.

"No, I am not ready," she said, "but this child is. I am bringing him because he is lame, and because he is hungry. Will you take him?" she asked.

"Yes," said the messenger, "and you, too. There is room at the King's table for both."

WINTER

THE GRAY HARE

A gray hare lived during the winter near a village. When night came, he would prick up one ear and listen, then he would prick up the other, jerk his whiskers, snuff, and sit up on his hind legs.

Then he would give one leap, two leaps, through the snow, and sit up again on his hind legs and look all around.

On all sides nothing was to be seen except snow. The snow lay in billows and glittered like silver. Above the hare was frosty vapor, and through this vapor glistened the big white stars.

The hare was obliged to make a long circuit across the highway to reach his favorite granary. On the highway he could hear the creaking of the sledges, the whinnying of horses, the groaning of the seats in the sledges.

Once more the hare paused near the road. The peasants were walking alongside of their sledges, with their coat collars turned up. Their faces were scarcely visible. Their beards, their eyebrows were white. Steam came from their mouths and noses.

Their horses were covered with sweat, and the sweat grew white with hoar frost. The horses strained on their collars, plunged into the hollows, and came up out of them again. Two old men were walking side by side, and one was telling the other how a horse had been stolen from him.

As soon as the teams had passed, the hare crossed the road, and leaped unconcernedly toward the threshing-floor. A little dog belonging to the teams caught sight of the hare and began to bark, and darted after him.

The hare made for the threshing-floor across the snowdrifts. But the depth of the snow impeded the hare, and even the dog, after a dozen leaps, sank deep in the snow and gave up the chase.

The hare also stopped, sat on his hind legs, and then proceeded at his leisure toward the threshing-floor.

On the way across the field he fell in with two other hares. They were nibbling and playing. The gray hare joined his mates, helped them clear away the icy snow, ate a few seeds of winter wheat, and then went on his way.

In the village it was all quiet; the fires were out; the only sound on the street was a baby crying in a cottage, and the framework of the houses creaking under the frost.

The hare hastened to the threshing-floor, and there he found some of his mates. He played with them on the well-swept floor, ate some oats from the tub on which they had already begun, mounted the snow-covered roof into the granary, and then went through the hedge toward his hole.

In the east the dawn was already beginning to redden, the stars dwindled, and the frosty vapor grew thicker over the face of the earth. In the neighboring village the women woke up and went out after water; the peasants began carrying fodder from the granaries; the children were shouting. Along the highway more and more teams passed by, and the peasants talked in louder tones.

The hare leaped across the road, went to his old hole, selected a place a little higher up, dug away the snow, curled into the depths of his new hole, stretched his ears along his back, and went to sleep with his eyes wide open.

THE SNOW IMAGE

One afternoon of a cold winter's day, two children asked leave of their mother to run out and play in the new-fallen snow. The older child was a little girl, so tender and modest that every one called her Violet. The boy was called Peony because of his fat, round face which made everybody think of sunshine and scarlet flowers.

The children lived in the city and had no wider play place than a little garden before the house, divided from the street by a white fence. The pear and plum trees, and the rose bushes in front of the parlor window were covered with white, with here and there an icicle for the fruit. It was a pleasant place to play. Their mother bundled them up in woolen jackets and wadded sacks, and a pair of striped gaiters on each little pair of legs, and worsted mittens on their hands. Out they ran, with a hop-skip-and-jump, into the heart of a huge snowdrift. When they had frosted one another all over with handfuls of snow, Violet had a new idea.

"Let us make an image out of snow," she said. "It shall be our little sister and shall run about and play with us all winter long!"

"Oh, yes!" cried Peony. "And mother shall see it."

"Yes," Violet answered. "Mother shall see the new little girl. But she must not make her come into the warm parlor, for our little snow sister will not love the warmth."

So the children began this great business of making a snow image that should run about. Violet told Peony what to do, while with her own careful fingers she shaped all the nicer parts of the snow figure. It seemed, in fact, not so much to be made by the children as to grow up under their hands as they were playing and talking about it. Their mother, who was sitting at the window, watched them. The longer she looked, the more and more surprised she grew.

"What remarkable children mine are!" she said to herself. "What other children could have made anything so like a little girl's figure out of snow at the first trial?"

"Peony, Peony!" cried Violet to her brother, "bring me some of that fresh snow from the farthest corner where we have not been trampling. I want to make our little snow sister's dress with it. You know it must be white, just as it came out of the sky."

"Here it is, Violet!" Peony said as he came floundering through the drifts. "Here is the snow for her dress. Oh, Violet, how beautiful she begins to look!"

"Yes," Violet said thoughtfully and quietly, "our snow sister does look very lovely. I did not know, Peony, that we could make such a sweet little girl as this. Now bring me those light wreaths of snow from the lower branches of the pear tree. You can climb up on a snowdrift and reach them. I must have them to make some curls for our little snow sister's head."

"Here they are, Violet," answered the little boy. "Take care you do not break them. Oh, how pretty!"

"We must have some shining little bits of ice to make the brightness of her eyes. She is not finished yet," Violet went on.

"Here they are," cried Peony. "Mother, mother! Look out and see what a nice little girl we have made!"

Their mother put down her work for an instant and looked out of the window. She was dazzled by the sun that had sunk almost to the edge of the world so she could not see the garden very distinctly. Still, through all the brightness of the sun and the snow, she saw a strange, small white figure in the garden. Peony was bringing fresh snow, and Violet was moulding it as a sculptor adds clay to his model.

"They do everything better than other children," their mother thought. "No wonder they make better snow images."

She sat down again to her work, and Violet and Peony talked about what a nice playmate their little snow sister would be for them all winter. Suddenly Violet called out joyfully:

"Look, Peony! Come quickly! A light has been shining on her cheek from that rose-colored cloud, and the color does not go away."

"And look, Violet!" Peony answered. "Oh, look at her hair! It is all like gold."

"Oh, of course," Violet said. "That color, you know, comes from the golden clouds. She is almost finished now. But her lips must be very red. Let us kiss them, Peony!"

Just then there came a breeze of the pure west wind blowing through the garden. It sounded so wintry cold that the mother was about to tap on the window pane to call the children in, when they both cried out to her with one voice:

"Mother, mother! We have finished our little snow sister and she is running about the garden with us!"

"They make me almost as much of a child as they," the mother said. "I can almost believe now that the snow image has really come to life." She went to the door and looked all over the garden. There was no gleam or dazzle now on it and she could see very well. What do you think she saw there?

Why, if you will believe me, there was a small figure of a girl dressed all in white, with rosy cheeks and golden curls, playing with Violet and Peony. She was none of the neighboring children. Not one had so sweet a face. Her dress fluttered in the breeze; she danced about in tiny white slippers. She was like a flying snowdrift.

"Who is this child?" the mother asked. "Does she live near us?"

Violet laughed that her mother could not understand so clear a matter. "This is our little snow sister," she said, "whom we have just been making."

At that instant a flock of snowbirds came flitting through the air. As was very natural, they avoided Violet and Peony. But—and this looked strange—they flew at once to the white-robed child, lighted on her shoulder, and seemed to claim her as their friend.

The little snow image was as glad to see these birds, old Winter's grandchildren, as they were to see her, and she welcomed them by holding out both of her hands. They tried to all alight on her ten small fingers and thumbs, crowding one another with a great fluttering of wings. One snowbird nestled close to her heart and another put its bill to her lips.

Just then the garden gate was thrown open and the children's father came in. A fur cap was drawn down over his ears and the thickest of gloves covered his hands. He had been working all day and was glad to get home. He smiled as he saw the children and their mother. His heart was tender, but his head was as hard and impenetrable as one of the iron pots that he sold in his hardware shop. At once, though, he perceived the little white stranger, playing in the garden, like a dancing snow wraith with the flock of snowbirds fluttering around her head.

"What little girl is that," he asked, "out in such bitter weather in a flimsy white gown and those thin slippers?"

"I don't know," the mother said. "The children say she is nothing but a snow image that they have been making this afternoon."

As she said this, the mother glanced toward the spot where the children's snow image had been made. There was no trace of it—no piled-up heap of snow—nothing save the prints of little footsteps around a vacant space!

"Nonsense!" said the father in his kind, matter-of-fact way. "This little stranger must be brought in out of the snow. We will take her into the parlor, and you shall give her a supper of warm bread and milk and make her as comfortable as you can."

But Violet and Peony seized their father by the hand.

"No," they cried. "This is our little snow girl, and she needs the cold west wind to breathe."

Their mother spoke, too. "There is something very strange about this," she said. "Could it be a miracle come to the children through their faith in their play?"

The father laughed. "You are as much a child as Violet and Peony," he said. Then he reached out his hand to draw the snow child into the house.

As he approached the snowbirds took to flight. He followed the snow child into a corner where she could not possibly escape. It was wonderful how she gleamed and sparkled and seemed to shed a glow all around her. She glistened like a star, or like an icicle in the moonlight.

"Come, you odd little thing," cried the honest man, seizing the snow child by her hand. "I have caught you at last and will make you comfortable in spite of yourself. We will put a nice new pair of stockings on your feet and you shall have a warm shawl to wrap yourself in. Your poor little nose, I am afraid, is frost bitten. But we will make it all right. Come along in."

So he led the snow child toward the house. She followed him, drooping and reluctant. All the glow and sparkle were gone from her.

"After all," said the mother, "she does look as if she were made of snow."

A puff of the west wind blew against the snow child; she sparkled again like a star.

"That is because she is half frozen, poor little thing!" said the father. "Here we are where it is warm!"

Sad and drooping looked the little white maiden as she stood on the hearth rug. The heat of the stove struck her like a pestilence. She looked wistfully toward the windows and caught a glimpse, through its red curtains, of the snow-covered roofs, the frosty stars and the delicious intensity of the cold night.

The mother had gone in search of the shawl and stockings, and Violet and Peony looked with terror at their little snow sister.

"I am going to find her parents," said the father, but he had scarcely reached the gate when he heard the children scream. He saw their mother's white face at the window.

"There is no need of going for the child's parents," she said.

There was no trace of the little white maiden, unless it were a heap of snow which, while they were gazing at it, melted quite away upon the hearth rug.

"What a quantity of snow the children brought in on their feet," their father said at last. "It has made quite a puddle here before the stove."

The stove, through the isinglass of its door, seemed to grin like a red-eyed demon at the mischief which it had done, for the story of the snow image is one of those rare cases where common sense finds itself at fault.

THE FIRE THAT WOULD NOT BURN

There was great trouble in the white castle that stood at the top of the hill. The huge fire that had burned in the castle kitchen for years had suddenly gone out, and no one seemed to be able to light it again.

It was deep winter outside. The hill was white with snow, and the fountains in the castle garden looked like tall ladies dressed in white cloaks. From all the castle turrets there hung long icicles, and inside the castle, where the walls and the floor were made all of stone, it was so cold that every one was blowing on his fingers and saying that something must be done at once about starting the fire in the kitchen.

It had been the warmest and the most useful fire in the castle, always bright and glowing and cheerful. It made the big kettle sing, and it cooked the food, and painted pictures in the fireplace for the little Prince, who always sat in front of it before he went to bed. Some said that the fire needed a special kind of fuel to keep it burning, and others said that it had gone out because it was such a hard, cold winter. Still others said that the castle folk were quarreling so over matters of state that they made the castle too cold for any fire to burn. The King blew the bellows, and the Queen wrapped up the little Prince in a fur coat, and the Cook piled on more logs, but still the fire would not burn.

"Go down the hill road," the King at last commanded the Court Messenger, "and wherever you see a bright fire burning in one of the houses, go inside and ask for some coals to bring back to the castle. It may be that we can light our fire in this way."

So the Messenger, with a great iron lantern for holding the coals, started out in the bitter cold.

"A light for the castle fire!" he called as he went. "Who will give me some coals with which to light the castle fire?"

As the Messenger went on his way, a great many people heard him and they all wanted to have a share in lighting the fire at the castle. Some thought that to do this would bring them riches.

"Here are glowing coals for you," said Gerald, whose father kept the forest; "and tell the King that we want as many gold pieces as there are lumps of coal in return, and some extra ones if he will add them."

So the Messenger put Gerald's red coals with the tongs inside his lantern, and he started back to the castle. He had gone only a few steps, though, when he saw that the coals had turned cold and gray, so he had to throw them beside the road and search farther.

A bright light shone from the fire in Gilda's house. Gilda's father was one of the King's guards and when she heard the Messenger's call, "A light for the castle fire!" she opened the door and asked him to come in.

"Fill your lantern with our coals," Gilda said, "and they will surely light the fire in the castle. Tell the King, though, that in return for the coals he must make my father Captain of the guards."

The Messenger took the coals and started back to the castle. He had gone but a little way, though, when he saw that the coals from Gilda's fire were no longer burning but had turned to gray ashes. So he emptied them out in the snow and went on down the hill. But his search was a hard one. So few of the coals that he was given would burn, and so few people wanted to give them freely.

At last he came to a tiny house on a bleak side of the hill. The wind blew down through the old chimney, and the frost had crept in through the cracks in the wall. The door opened at once when he knocked, though, and inside he found a little girl, stirring porridge over a small fire.

"A light for the castle fire?" she repeated when the Messenger had told her what he wanted. "You may have as many coals as you like, although we have few large ones. I am my father's housewife and I tend this small fire so that the kitchen may be comfortable for him when he comes home from work. I am cooking his supper, too," she said. "But do you sit down and warm yourself, and have a bowl of warm supper before you start out in the cold again. Then you may have half of our fire if the King needs it."

The Messenger did as the little girl bade him, and then he lifted one small, bright coal from the fire, and put it in his lantern.

"It will never burn all the way back to the castle," he said to himself, but with each step the coal grew brighter. It cast pink shadows on the snow as if the spring were sending wild roses up through the ground. It made the dark road in front of the Messenger as bright as if the sun were shining, and it warmed him like the summer time. When he came to the castle, the coal still burned and glowed. As soon as he touched it to the gray logs in the fireplace they burst into flames, and the castle fire was kindled again.

They wondered why the new fire made the kettle sing so much more sweetly than it had ever sung before, and warmed the hearts of the castle folk so that they forgot to quarrel. At last, when they talked it over with the

Messenger, they decided that it was because love had come from the cottage with the coal, and was kindled and burning now in the castle fire.

CHRISTMAS

THE CHILD WHO SAW SANTA CLAUS

There was, once upon a time, a child who wanted very much to see Santa Claus; just as every other child has always wanted to see him.

So the Child listened at the chimney for Santa Claus, and watched for him when sleighs flew by over the snowy streets, and wanted to touch his rosy cheeks and his red cloak trimmed with white fur.

"I am old enough now to see Santa Claus," the Child said. That was quite true, because he was seven years old. "Show him to me, mother," he begged.

"Oh, I cannot do that," the Child's mother said. "I can tell you about Santa Claus but I cannot show you his face."

"May I go out and look for Santa Claus, myself, then?" the Child asked. "This is the day before Christmas and if I do not see him to-day, you know I shall have to wait a whole year."

"Yes, you may go out and look for Santa Claus," the Child's mother said, and she brought him his warm coat and cap and his red mittens; "but do not go too far away from home, for Santa Claus stays very close to the homes where there are children on Christmas Eve," she added.

So the Child started out. He was very sure that he would know Santa Claus when he saw him. Ever since he was a very little boy he had seen pictures of Santa Claus. He would be a jolly, fat little old man with twinkling eyes and a nose like a cherry. He would wear a long red cloak and, perhaps, he would be in his toy shop making toys, of which he would give the child a great many. Or he would be driving his sleigh full of toys through the city, and the Child would know that he was coming by the tinkling sound of his silver bells.

At the gate the Child met his grandfather. He was a very old man with white hair and spectacles. But he could play horse as well as the Child, and all the Child's nicest toys, the stone blocks, and the train with tracks, and all the rest, his grandfather had given him. Now, his grandfather's arms were full of fat, mysterious parcels. One parcel bulged as if it were a toy fire engine, and another parcel bulged as if it were a baseball mask, and a ball, and gloves.

"Where are you going?" the Child's grandfather asked.

"I am going to see Santa Claus," the Child answered.

The grandfather smiled until his blue eyes shone. "Will you know Santa Claus when you see him?" he asked.

"Oh, yes," the Child said. "Santa Claus is an old man with white hair, and twinkling eyes, and a nose like a cherry —" but the Child suddenly stopped.

"Oho!" his grandfather laughed, and the Child listened in surprise. He had never heard such a merry laugh before. His grandfather rubbed his nose that the cold had painted as red as a cherry. Then his grandfather was gone, and the Child went on, wondering.

The streets were full of people, their arms crowded with big white parcels tied with red ribbon. Some of them carried great green wreaths and bunches of holly. There were so many grocery teams, and toy shop teams, and flower shop teams that the Child was afraid to cross the street. He went part of the way across. Then he saw the horses coming, and he did not know which way to go. He might have been hurt, but a kind hand took hold of his and helped him safely across the street. He looked up at the man, who wore a long red cloak trimmed with white.

"Who are you?" the Child asked.

"One of the Christmas helpers," the man said. "I stand here at the street corner and ring a Christmas bell, and people who pass by give me money for my poor ones. And where are you going?" he asked the Child.

"I am going to see Santa Claus," the Child answered.

"Will you know Santa Claus when you see him?" the man asked.

"Oh, yes," the Child said. "Santa Claus wears a long red cloak trimmed with white —" But then the Child stopped.

The man pulled his red cloak about him. It was very cold and he had no fire. Then he took his place at the street corner again. The Child watched him and then went on, wondering.

A little farther on, there was an old man, sitting in a shop, and making toys. Once he had been a soldier, but now he was able to do nothing but sit at his work bench carving, and gluing, and painting playthings for children. The Child went in and watched him work. There were wooly lambs that would bleat, and toy horses with harnesses on the shelves of the toy shop. There were dolls with blue eyes, and dolls with brown eyes, and dolls that could talk, and dolls that could walk, all waiting there for Christmas Eve. The toyman, himself, was fitting wheels on wooden carts and wheelbarrows, and as he worked he sang a quaint little tune with these words,

"A little green tree,From a far white hill,Made a Christmas tree,By my merry skill—"

Then the toyman, who used to be a soldier, turned to the Child who was just going out of the shop. "Where are you going?" the toyman asked the Child.

"I am going to see Santa Claus," the Child answered.

"Will you know Santa Claus when you see him?" the toyman asked.

"Oh, yes," the Child said. "Santa Claus will be making toys—" but he did not say any more, for the toyman got down from his bench and put a box of quaintly carved little wooden animals in the Child's happy hands. It was a good gift, for each animal was different, and it had taken the toyman many evenings to cut them out.

"Merry Christmas to you from Santa Claus!" said the toyman, as the Child thanked him and went on, wondering.

Now it was Christmas Eve, and so the Child started home. The lights from the Christmas candles shining from many windows made a bright path for him, and he felt very happy indeed. He knew how pleasant it would be at home. The Christmas tree would be set up, waiting for the gifts that each one was going to give the others. There would be a fire of new logs in the fireplace, and holly wreaths at the windows, and he would hang up his stocking. The Child felt as glad as if Santa Claus were walking home by his side through the snowy street, but he thought, just before he reached home,

"I wish that I could hear Santa Claus' bells!"

Then the Child stopped, and listened. He heard, coming toward him on the frosty air, the sound of many silver-toned bells. The Christmas star had shone out in the sky as soon as the sun set. Now the church bells were ringing, some near and some far, to welcome the Holy Child of Christmas Eve. Their chiming was as wonderful as the sound of the strings of silver bells on Santa Claus' sleigh.

"I shall know Santa Claus by the sound of his bells," the Child repeated to himself.

Then he came home, and his mother was very glad to have him back.

"Did you see Santa Claus?" she asked.

"Oh, yes!" the Child answered, for he was quite sure about it now. "I saw him when I met grandfather, and I saw him standing in a red cloak at the street corner and helping the poor. I saw him in the toyman's shop, and I heard his bells ringing just now. I saw Santa Claus everywhere," the Child said.

And so may every child see Santa Claus, wherever love and goodness are at the blessed Christmas time.

THE CHRISTMAS GARDEN

None of the children in the village would play with Christopher because he was the child of Beggar Mother of the Göinge Forest.

The Forest was deep, full of brown, leafless oaks and green fir trees, with the wind singing shrill tunes in their branches. In the darkest part was a thick mountain wall, and in the wall there was an old door made of rough boards. The village children, gathering cones in the Forest, had peeped through this door when Christopher had left it open a crack.

"Christopher's home is nothing but a cave with stones for the floor!" the children whispered.

"Beggar Mother stirs a pot that hangs over a fire of logs!" they said.

"Christopher and his little brothers and sisters wear skins for clothing. They sleep, like wolves, on beds of pine and moss!" they said, too, and then they ran away when they saw Christopher coming out.

He was as roughly dressed as one of the baby bears whom he knew in the Göinge Forest and for whom he gathered wild honey; or as shy as one of the little red foxes that had no home save a hollow tree. All his life he had been hungry, and starved, and scorned. But Christopher was known by all of the Forest as loving and gentle and unselfish.

Beggar Mother neither baked nor brewed, but when she went her way down to the village from door to door with all her little ones clinging to her skirts, the villagers would sometimes give her six brown loaves, one for each of her children.

Then Christopher would creep out of the cave and break his bread to give some crumbs to the starlings, the finches, and the baby squirrels. He knew where the wild strawberries grew, and he gathered them for his mother. He pulled grass and leaves for the wild hares. He had once lifted Mother Fox from her trap and sent her back to her babies. He brought spring water from the rocks for the flowers, and never frightened the owls or caught the butterflies.

But the Göinge Forest was cold and asleep now, for it was Christmas time.

Christopher knew that it was now Christmas Eve for he had been to the village and looked in the doors. Lighted candles were being set in the windows. Great pieces of bread and meat were being placed on the tables, and bunches of grain thick with seeds were hung in the gardens to be a Christmas feast for the birds.

But when the villagers saw Christopher from the cave in the Forest looking in their doors, they slammed them shut, for they knew him only as the child of Beggar Mother. They had no room for him on Christmas Eve.

So Christopher walked alone and he came, through the snow, to the little church on the edge of the Göinge Forest. Brother Anselmo tended the church. He had arranged the little crèche, which was like the stable where the Holy Child lay on the first Christmas Eve. There was the manger, the gilt star suspended over it, and the toy cattle that Brother Anselmo had carved from wood with his own hands. He had trimmed the church with greens. Now, Brother Anselmo was ready to ring the bell, but he had not the strength. He was a very old man and the bell was heavy. The rope was stiff with ice, and snow blinded him in the belfry.

Christopher knew Brother Anselmo very well. In the summer he helped him tend his garden of herbs, and in the winter he brought him fagots. With his bare feet Christopher climbed up to the belfry. With his little hands he pulled with all his might at the frozen bell rope. Then the bell rang out more sweetly than ever before to tell the village and the Forest that it was Christmas Eve.

But a strange thing happened. As Christopher rang the Christmas bell once, the trees in the Forest covered themselves with green leaves, and the ground was no longer bare, but bright with flowers. A flock of starlings flew to the top of a fir tree and stopped there, singing. Their feathers glittered with gold and red like jewels, for they were Paradise starlings.

Christopher rang the bell a second time, and the baby squirrels began playing among the mosses. There was the smell of newly plowed fields. The tinkle of sheep and cow bells could be heard, and the pine and spruce trees covered themselves with red cones, like kings in crimson mantles.

When Christopher rang the bell a third time, the wild strawberries began covering the ground, red and ripe. Butterflies as large as lilies flew through the air, and a bee-hive in a hollow oak dripped with golden honey. A light like that of noon time in summer streamed down. The air was soft and warm, and white doves flew through the Forest singing.

The villagers saw the wonder and they came, running, to the Forest. The Christmas bell was ringing, but winter was gone. The Forest had blossomed more beautifully than they had ever known it to in summer.

"What has brought this wonder?" they asked. Then they saw Christopher coming home. Wherever he walked the ground glowed with more flowers, and the birds and butterflies lighted on his shoulders, and hands, and there seemed to be music coming down from the sky.

The whole Göinge Forest was a Christmas garden for Christopher whom they had turned away from their doors. They understood that, now, because the next morning the Forest was again white with snow and asleep for the winter.

THE CHRISTMAS TREE IN THE BARN

Billy and Betty had the beautiful plan about having a Christmas tree in the barn. They were spending the winter with father and mother on Uncle William's big farm, and they loved every one of the barn creatures very much indeed.

There were the hens who gave them such fine fresh eggs, and Shep, the dog, who kept the lambs safe on the hill in the summer time. There was Bessie, Uncle William's horse, who took them for picnic rides and to church. There was Peter, the barn cat, who kept the mice away from the vegetables and grain that was stored in the barn.

"They are all so kind to us, and they ought to have a Christmas, Billy," Betty said.

"We will go right out in the woods and cut them a Christmas tree," Billy said.

They found a little spruce tree that was so small they could cut it easily, and they dragged it to the barn on their sled. Uncle William gave them a green wooden pail that they filled with sand to hold the animals' Christmas tree, and they stood it in the middle of the barn floor. It was such fun trimming it!

Betty picked bright red berries in the woods and fastened them with pins to the ends of the branches, and Billy made some little scarlet wreaths to hang on them. He strung cranberries on some fine wire and fastened it in a circle to make these wreaths. Then they cut snowflakes from white paper and fastened them to the twigs, just as if they had fallen there from the sky.

But hanging the animals' Christmas presents on their tree was the most fun of all.

Betty cut some little Christmas stockings from tarlatan, seamed them with red worsted, and filled them with yellow corn for the hens. She tied lumps of sugar with red ribbon and hung apples on, too, for Bessie. Shep had two juicy marrow bones tied with big red bows, but neither Billy nor Betty could decide what Peter, the barn cat, would like for a Christmas present. There did not seem to be anything that Peter really needed, for he had two collars, and three balls, and all the milk he could drink.

They had not decided what to give Peter on Christmas morning, and it seemed too bad, for when Billy and Betty went out to the barn each creature seemed to be enjoying the tree very much. The hens were clucking, Bessie was neighing, and Shep was walking round and round the tree, smelling of his bones. And there sat Peter, right under the tree, and looking up into its green branches.

"Poor Peter!" Betty said, "with no Christmas present."

But just then Peter jumped right up into the Christmas tree in the barn and came down with a little gray mouse in his mouth! The mouse had been nibbling the corn in the Christmas stockings, but Peter thought it was his Christmas gift. So the tree was quite perfect, and all the barn enjoyed it very much indeed.

PATRIOTISM

THE RESCUE OF OLD GLORY

When mother was making plans for a "safe and sane Fourth," Uncle Henry said, "Why not take the children to the park and have a kite party? I'll help them make the kites."

The next morning Harry and Anna were busy out on the piazza with Uncle Henry. By ten o'clock three handsome white kites were drying in a row. Anna called them the "Big Bear, the Middle-Sized Bear, and the Baby Bear."

When the kites were dry, the whole family started for the park — Uncle Henry with the Big Bear and a box of luncheon, Harry with the Middle-Sized Bear, and Anna, of course, with the Baby Bear. Mother carried some sewing and grandmother carried the surprise, something that Uncle Henry had brought home in a flat box. When they reached the park, they found a French society holding a picnic. A tent was up, the band was playing, the older boys were shooting at a target, and the little boys and girls were flying red and blue balloons.

Uncle Henry said, "Ladies first, always," and he soon had the Baby Bear in the air, and the string in Anna's hands. He drove the bobbin into the ground, to make sure that the kite would not get away. Harry insisted upon putting his kite up alone. Then Uncle Henry put up the Big Bear, and when it was up some distance, he asked grandmother to open the box. Then he shook out a red-white-and-blue silk American flag, and the crowd cheered.

Uncle Henry tied the flag to a loop of string, and fastened it to the Big Bear's string. Then he let it out, hand over hand. Up, up, went Old Glory, and snapped in the breeze. The higher it went, the farther out the kite soared, until it hung over the harbor. They were all so busy watching it that they had not seen that the picnic people below were pointing up to the flag; but when the band struck up the Star-Spangled Banner, and the foreign people began to sing, Uncle Henry noticed one dark-skinned boy who sang with a strange accent and great energy, and who kept his big, solemn eyes on the flag that glowed against the sky. But when the boy, whose name was Caspar, saw the others looking at him, he ran down the hill and hid behind the children.

"Any one who can sing the Star-Spangled Banner like that is a good American," said Uncle Henry, as he drove his bobbin into the ground, and prepared to open the box of luncheon.

When the foreigners went in to dinner, Caspar did not follow. He took his sandwiches, frosted cake, and ice-cream, and sat down on the grass, where he could look at the flag.

There was not a child in the whole park who loved the Stars and Stripes as little Caspar did, not even the two American children; for in his own country Caspar had lived in a mission house, where they had told him all about America, and how the Stars and Stripes protected the people, even the poorest of little children. They told him that he must never harm the flag, or allow it to be trampled on. After he came to America, his teacher had taught him to salute the flag.

He had heard the flag song on the big ship, and he felt that it was Old Glory that had brought him safe to one of his own country-women in America, with whom he lived.

Caspar was thinking of all this as he lay on the grass, and saw the flag fluttering in the light wind. He had watched it for some time, when he saw it give a quick little shiver, then begin to sink slowly, and then faster. He looked to the end of the line, and saw that the great white kite was dipping about in a strange manner; then he looked up to the hill and saw the kite man leaping down the slope as fast as he could. The American children were running behind him.

Caspar trembled with excitement. What would happen to the flag? Would it get trampled upon, or would it go out to sea and get wet and spoiled? Oh, he must help them get Old Glory! He ran until he was directly beneath the flag; then he stretched his arms high to catch it if it fell. But a strong breeze came up, and carried the Big Bear over the water, and pulled the flag with it. Caspar ran on to the water's edge.

Caspar did not know what to do next. There were no people on the shore, and no boats were near. The flag had not been trampled on, but it might fall in the water any minute. Where were the people? Did they know that a great calamity was about to happen, to everybody in the park, to everybody in America, perhaps to the mission ladies who had been so good to him? How could the people sit about, eating and drinking, when there was such trouble in the world? He cried out to Uncle Henry and the children, who were now quite near, strange and broken words, and he tried to tell them that he could not swim.

"Good boy, swim for it! You'll get it!" shouted Uncle Henry.

Caspar understood the word "swim," but not the rest. He thought the kite man must be telling him that he could not swim, either. He looked out to the flag; it was surely going into the water; it flapped and dipped, then dipped deeper still, right into the water. Caspar did not wait another minute. Off went his jacket, and with a wild look toward the shore, he ran into the water. His feet slipped on the sandy bottom, and the kite jerked up, then down, then up — but it was always just out of reach.

They watched the boy, who was trying hard to keep the flag in sight.

"Hurry, hurry, Uncle Henry, he can't swim a stroke!" shouted Harry.

Uncle Henry was just in time; Caspar had a firm hold on Old Glory, and came up tangled in its folds.

After Uncle Henry had shaken the water out of the boy, he sat him on his shoulder, where everybody could see him. "Now, one, two, three!" he said, as he waved his free arm. "All cheer for the boy who would not let the flag be lost even if he couldn't swim! Hoo-ray!"

"Hoo-ray! hoo-ray! hoo-ray!" they said; and then they cheered all over again, and crowded round Uncle Henry and Caspar until the pair started home to put on dry clothes.

When little Caspar went home that night, he carried the flag that he had saved. Grandmother had washed and dried it, and it looked as good as new.

THE LOG CABIN BOY

How would you like to have begun life in a little log cabin set in the midst of a western wilderness? Suppose, too, that the cabin had no window and so many cracks that it let in the winter winds and even the snow!

That was how little Abe first saw life a long time ago, in February of 1809. It was rough life for a small boy. Even his mother had to know how to shoot, for the cabin was in the woods where wild beasts and Indians surrounded it. There was nothing to eat except what Abe's father raised or hunted. They had nothing to wear except the cloth his mother spun and wove, or the skins of animals.

By the time little Abe was six years old, though, he had learned more than a boy of that age to-day. He could fish and hunt. He was not afraid of Indians. He could catch hold of a sycamore tree on the edge of the brook outside the cabin, and swing himself way across the brook.

But little Abe's father was not satisfied with his boy's knowing only how to live an outdoor life. He could not read himself, but it was his great longing that little Abe should have this knowledge.

It was when Abe was seven years old and his sister, Sarah, a year younger, that their father spoke about this.

"I want the children to learn to read," he said. "There is a man in a shanty down the road who knows how. He can't write, but he could teach Abe and Sarah their letters."

So the two little folks started off, Abe in a linsey-woolsey suit, buckskin breeches, and a coonskin cap. It was a long walk, and the children had only hoe cake to carry for their dinner, but they were strong and sturdy. They were clever, too. In a few weeks, Abe knew as much as the school-master. Then he began to wish, oh, so much, that he had some books to read at home in the cabin.

There was a Bible at home, an old catechism, and a spelling book. Abe read these over and over again in the dim candle light of the cabin. One day his father surprised him. He brought him a new book. It was Pilgrim's Progress, the most wonderful story, little Abe thought, that he had ever read. It was only a borrowed book; books cost a very great deal of money in those long-ago days, more than Mr. Lincoln could pay. He was able to borrow more, though. Little Abe read Æsop's fables, and he liked them so much that he learned the stories by heart. He could tell the fable of the Hare and the Tortoise, the Crow and the Pitcher, and many others.

It made Abe so happy to have these books that he made up his mind to try to do something, in return, to surprise his father. It was spring of the year and Abe and his father were plowing, turning up the soft brown earth, ready for the new seeds. Mr. Lincoln missed his boy. He looked back, and what do you think he saw? Abe had spelled with a stick, in the soft brown earth, his own name. His father had not known that he could write, but there were the letters as plainly outlined as if they had been in a copy book: ABRAHAM LINCOLN.

He had taught himself to write by practising in the snow, and making letters on the logs of the cabin walls with pieces of charcoal.

A great deal began to happen now to Abraham, although he was only eight years old. His father decided to travel a hundred miles from Kentucky to a new farm in Indiana to see if he might not be a little more prosperous. There were no railroads. There was not even a stage route. They packed their bedding on two horses and set out on the journey overland. It took seven days, sleeping on the ground under the stars at night. And when they reached the new home, there was not even a shelter waiting for them. A road had been cut through the forests, but all the clearing was yet to be done.

Abraham had an axe of his own and he went to work with it. He was a true pioneer boy, and not one bit afraid of work. He cut poles while his father laid the foundations of the new cabin. They were only able to put up a "half-faced" camp at first, with three sides and one side open. And it was hard work. The great, unhewn logs had to be all notched and fitted together, and the cracks filled in with clay. They made a loft, and fitted in a door and a window. Abraham learned how to make a table and some stools. Then, after the bitter winter was over, the spring brought them more comfort and happiness. The corn and vegetables they planted came up, and Abraham had a little time to read again.

He had a new book, now, that a neighbor had let him take. It was the story of a boy who had, also, in his little boy days, an axe like Abraham's; but he had used it to cut down his father's cherry tree. When he had grown to be a man, though, he was our Great American. Abraham took this book, the Life of George Washington, to bed with him and read it when the snow was sifting in through the cabin roof and over his quilt. He read the book many times.

"What are you going to be when you grow up?" the neighbor asked Abraham.

"I am going to be the President of the United States," the boy replied.

Every one thought this a very good joke, for Abraham was growing up now. He had legs that were too long for his body and it was the same way with his arms. He was almost six feet tall although he was not yet fifteen years old. His head, set on top of his long neck, looked almost out of place. People laughed when they compared him with other Presidents of the United States.

Abraham kept his thought in his mind, though, and he went on working, and reading when he had time in the fire light of the long winter evenings. As he threshed, and chopped, and plowed, he could not help dreaming a little. All his life he had worked hard for others, and he really liked this kind of work more than any other. He wanted to go on helping others, only in a greater, broader way.

We all know what happened to Abraham Lincoln. His dream came true. He was our noblest President and carried on his broad shoulders the burdens of the slaves. It was a long road from the little log cabin in Kentucky to the White House at Washington, but President Lincoln, himself, tells us how he made the journey.

He was visiting, once, a hospital full of wounded soldiers. There were several thousand of them, and each one of them loved Mr. Lincoln so that he wanted to shake hands with him. He took and held the hand of each. It was enough to cripple an ordinary man, but Mr. Lincoln's kind, plain face was smiling when some one asked if he were tired.

"Oh, no," he said. "The hardships of my boyhood made me strong."

Very likely, too, it was the struggles of learning to write on bare boards and in the earth that helped Abraham Lincoln to write his name in letters of gold on our history pages.

THEIR FLAG

The flag had been in the family for years, and years, and years. Great-grandfather Wolcott had carried it, and Grandfather Wolcott had hung it on a pole in front of his farm house. Father Wolcott had taken it to Boston to be mended when he was a young man, and it hung in front of Billy and Betty Wolcott's piazza now every day. Father took the flag in at night, and Billy and Betty folded it very carefully in the old creases, and mother put it out on the piazza the first thing in the morning.

The whole family was very proud indeed of the flag.

There was going to be a wonderful parade on Washington's Birthday. Every one in town was looking forward to seeing it. The Home Guard, the firemen, the policemen, the Old Veterans, the Red Cross, and the Boy Scouts would parade. There would be several brass bands, fifes and drums, and trumpets. Whoever had a flag would hang it as high as possible, and the beautiful stars and stripes of Old Glory floated from the town hall, and the school houses, and the churches.

The day before Washington's Birthday something happened at the Wolcotts' house. The telegraph office telephoned to say that father couldn't come home until the day after to-morrow. He was detained on business in Boston. All day it had rained. The flag was not out on the piazza, so it did not matter about that, but Billy and Betty were so sorry not to have father to go with them to the parade.

The morning of Washington's Birthday something else happened. Grandmother sent mother a letter asking if she would come over to Greendale and help her entertain the company; ever so many of the relatives were coming to spend the holiday with her, more than she expected.

So Betty held mother's coat for her, and Billy telephoned for a cab to take her down to the station.

"Be good children and don't disturb cook; she will be very busy to-day," mother said as she kissed Billy and Betty good-bye. It was not until she had gone that they thought of what had happened to them.

"We can't go to the parade," Betty said.

"Our flag isn't out!" Billy said.

"We must put it out ourselves then," Betty said, but that was not very easy to do.

The Wolcott flag was very large and very tender because it was so old. It had to be handled with great care, and Billy and Betty were not very big.

"We must hang it all ourselves because it is the flag of our country," Billy said. So they carried it out to the piazza, and unfolded it there very, very carefully.

"Now how are we going to get it up to the top of the piazza?" Betty asked.

There were three hooks on the edge of the piazza roof and three loops on the flag, but father could only just reach, standing on a chair, to put the loops on the hooks.

"The step ladder!" Billy said. "I'll climb up on that."

"And I'll reach the flag up to you on the broom!" Betty said.

So Billy and Betty, together, brought the step ladder and set it up on the piazza. Then Billy climbed up, and Betty reached up the flag on the broom so Billy could hook it into place. It was done at last. The wind took it, and the Stars and Stripes blew out over the lawn just as they should on Washington's Birthday.

"If we can't go to the parade, we can guard the flag here at home," Betty said. "Let's salute it, first."

So Billy and Betty saluted Old Glory, just as they had been taught to in school. Then Billy brought down his drum and stood on one side of the flag, and Betty tied her red muffler over her blue coat for a belt, and put on her white tam-o'-shanter cap, and stood on the other side of the flag, playing that she was Liberty.

"Listen; what's that!" said Billy and Betty just then.

Oh, there was a crash of bands and the shouts of people as they cheered. Down the street came the parade in khaki, and blue, and red. The line of march had been changed and it was going by Billy's and Betty's house. They all saw the flag, and the band played the Star Spangled Banner as they passed.

Suppose the flag hadn't been up! The Home Guard knew all about how old it was. The Old Veterans knew that great-grandfather had carried it, and grandfather had hung it on a pole in front of his farm house. They knew that father had taken it to Boston once to be mended.

The secret was that nobody knew who had put the Wolcotts' flag out for Washington's Birthday.

SAINT VALENTINE'S DAY
THE VALENTINE BOX

Roger had planned to send a great many valentines to the girls and boys he knew. There were beautiful valentines in the toy shop window, red satin hearts in little heart-shaped boxes, painted post card valentines, and little card-board figures holding baskets of flowers.

Roger had been saving his allowance for four weeks and he was quite sure that he had enough money to buy a valentine for the little girl next door, and one for the little girl across the street, and one for the boy on the next block, and one for the boy who lived upstairs.

So, quite early the day before Saint Valentine's Day, Roger decided to go out and buy his valentines.

Just as he was about to start, though, he heard a sound from the playroom. Peep, peep, peep. Oh, it was Roger's pet canary who was calling to him, "Wait a moment, little master! You have forgotten to feed me."

Roger knew that he must not buy valentines if his pet bird was hungry. He found that it needed fresh water to drink, and the cage needed cleaning too. When he had done all this and filled the seed box, his mother called him.

"I want two yards more of lace like this for the baby's dress, Roger. Will you please go down to the store and buy it for me?"

"Oh, yes!" Roger said, for he thought that he should be able to go on down to the toy store and buy his valentines at the same time. But just as he was going out of the door his mother spoke again. "Come right home, Roger, just as quickly as you can. I want to finish the baby's dress so that she can wear it this afternoon when I take her over to Aunt Lucy's."

Roger got the lace and hurried home with it, but he couldn't get the valentines then. He had to amuse the baby while his mother sewed on the lace.

"I can go for the valentines this afternoon," Roger thought. But right after luncheon mother dressed the baby and started out for Aunt Lucy's house.

"I may not be back until five o'clock, Roger," his mother said as she kissed him good-bye. "You won't leave dear grandmother alone a minute, will you?"

"No, mother," Roger said, but he could have cried, for he knew now that he could not buy his valentines at all.

Grandmother lost her spectacles several times, and dropped her knitting ball several more times, and wanted Roger to take her for a walk, so he was very busy all the afternoon. He was glad to be busy for he felt very badly indeed about having no valentines to send. All the children to whom he had planned to send valentines had sent valentines to him the year before. The children were his loved playmates and he knew that Saint Valentine's Day was the holiday for telling one's love.

He did not let his dear grandmother know how sorry he was, though, and after a while it was five o'clock, and his mother came home.

"Has Roger been a good boy?" she asked his grandmother.

"As good as gold," grandmother said. "He has just warmed my heart all the afternoon."

"Well, I thought he would," his mother said. "Oh, I almost forgot something, Roger. I have a surprise for you up in the attic."

She went up to the attic and came back with a box in her hand.

"I meant to give these to you this morning, Roger," she said. "I found them in an old trunk when I was cleaning the attic last week. They are just as good as new and much prettier than the ones in the shops now, I think. They are the valentines that I had when I was a little girl."

Oh, such beautiful valentines as filled the valentine box! There were enough so that Roger could take one to every child in the neighborhood on the morning of Saint Valentine's Day.

His mother had been right about these pretty, old-fashioned valentines. They were nicer than any in the toy shop. Roger spread them all out on the library table, and looked at them. Suddenly he found out something queer about the valentines; they made him feel as if he had been playing Saint Valentine all day.

Some of the valentines had cunning little paper windows that pulled out and showed tiny gold birds inside. They made Roger think of his pet canary that he had fed that morning.

Some of the valentines were bordered and trimmed with gilt, and silver, and white paper lace. It made Roger think of the lace he had bought for his mother.

A great many of the valentines were in the shape of hearts, or there were hearts hung from them, or hearts on them that could be pulled out and would stand alone. They made Roger think of what his dear grandmother had said,

"Roger has warmed my heart all the afternoon."

"Hurrah for the valentine box!" Roger said as he began putting valentines in envelopes. He felt most unusually happy.

THE PRINCE'S VALENTINE

Once upon a time there was a little Prince, and he wanted to give a valentine to a little Princess who lived in a neighboring kingdom. She was a very beautiful little Princess indeed, for her smile was as bright as her golden hair, and her love for her subjects was as deep as the blue of her eyes.

"What kind of a valentine shall I get for the Princess?" the Prince asked.

"A heart, your Highness; nothing but a heart will do!" said the Court Wise Man.

"A beautiful heart, your Highness; nothing but a beautiful heart will do!" said the Court Ladies.

"A priceless heart, your Highness; nothing but a priceless heart will do!" said the Court Chancellor.

So the Prince started out to get a heart valentine for the little Princess that would be both beautiful and beyond price, and he did not know where to find it.

Before long, though, he came to a jeweller's shop that was full of pretty, costly things to wear. There were pins, and bracelets, and necklaces made of silver and gold, and set with rubies, and sapphires, and emeralds, and diamonds.

"This is the place to find a valentine for the little Princess," thought the Prince, and he selected a diamond heart hung on a gold chain as thin as a thread for the little Princess to wear about her neck.

The Prince gave the jeweller his bag of gold and started out of the shop with the diamond heart in his hand. But he stopped at the door, looking at the heart. It was dull, and no longer shining. What was the matter with it, he wondered. Then he remembered. It was not the right valentine for the little Princess because it had been bought with his bag of gold. So the Prince gave the diamond heart back to the jeweller, and went on again.

After the Prince had gone quite a distance he came to a pastry shop. It was full of delicious things to eat, jam tarts, and little strawberry pies, thickly frosted cakes, and plum buns. In the window of the pastry shop was a huge cake baked in the shape of a heart. It was rich with sugar and spices, and the icing on the top was almost as thick as the cake itself.

"This is the place to find the valentine for the little Princess!" thought the Prince, and he pointed to the great heart cake in the window. "How much must I pay for that cake?" he asked of the pastry cook.

"Oh, you could not buy that cake!" the pastry cook replied. "I made it as a decoration for the shop for Valentine's Day. But I will give it to you, your Highness."

So the Prince thanked the pastry cook, and started out of the shop with the great cake in his arms.

"This must surely be the valentine for the little Princess, because I could not buy it," he thought.

Then the Prince almost dropped the cake. It had suddenly grown too heavy for him to carry. What was the matter with the rich, huge cake, he wondered. Then he remembered. It was not the right valentine for the little Princess because something rich to eat is not beautiful. So the Prince gave the cake back to the pastry cook, and went on again.

Now he went a long, long way, and he came to a bird seller beside the road. He had little gold birds, and bright-colored ones in green basket cages. They were all singing as if their throats would burst, but the Prince could hear one soft note above the others, because it was so clear and sweet. It was the cooing of a little dove who sat in her cage apart from the others. The Prince thought he had never seen such a beautiful little dove, as white as snow, and with rose red feet.

"Why does she sing so much more sweetly than the others?" the Prince asked, pointing to the little white dove.

The bird seller smiled.

"She sings because of her heart," he said. "The other birds sing in the sunshine, but look"—he held up the dove's cage, and the Prince saw that the little white dove had closed, blind eyes. "She sings in the dark because of her happy heart," the bird seller said.

"May I buy her," the Prince asked, "to give as a valentine to a little Princess?"

"Oh, I will give her to you," the bird seller said. "Very few people want to take care of a blind bird."

But the little Princess did. She liked the white dove better than any of her other valentines. She hung her cage in a pink rose tree in the sunniest part of the garden, and she often invited the Prince to sit with her under the tree and listen to the dove's sweet song.

WHY THE DOVE IS ON OUR VALENTINES

A long time ago when there were no white men in our country, but only Indians who lived in the forest, there was a timid little Indian boy.

All the other Indian lads loved the dark, so full of stars, and moonlight; but this boy was afraid of the dark and did not venture out of his father's wigwam after the sun had set. The other Indian lads hunted bears, and sailed the swift rapids in frail birch-bark canoes, and had no fear of anything that ran, or stalked, or flew. But the Indian boy about which this story is told was afraid of all the wild creatures of the forest. He never ventured far away from the safe circle of his home campfire. Most of all was the boy afraid of Hoots, the bear.

This was because Hoots was a part of the forest. He hid himself by day, for he was afraid of bows and swift flying arrows. But at night, the bear prowled near the Indian camp, and could be heard from one end of the forest to the other, his great feet crunching through the dried bushes and twigs.

In those days the Indians believed that a good spirit, called the manito, watched over them, and guided them, and kept them from harm. The story tells that the manito was walking one day through the trees of the forest when he saw this little Indian boy, hiding behind a pine tree and giving loud cries of terror.

"What is this that I hear?" asked the manito. "No Indian boy ever cries. Come forth that I may see who the coward is, and learn of what he is afraid."

So the boy came out from behind the pine tree and spoke to the manito,

"I have been sent with my bow and arrows to hunt for food for my mother to cook," he said, "but I can go no farther in the forest. I am afraid of Hoots, the great bear, who lives in it."

"You should be afraid of nothing, my son, not even of Hoots, the bear," warned the manito.

"But I can't help being afraid of Hoots; I think that he may eat me," said the boy, and at that he began crying again, "Boo-hoo, boo-hoo."

"There shall be no coward among the Indians," said the manito. "And I see that you will always be afraid. I shall change your form into that of a bird.

Whenever any one looks at you, he will say, 'There is the bird that is the most timid of all.'"

As the manito finished speaking, the Indian boy's deerskin cloak fell to the ground; his bow and arrows dropped too, for he had no longer any hands with which to hold them. He was suddenly completely covered with a coat of soft gray feathers. His moccasins fell off, and his feet turned into the wee feet of a bird. He wanted to call his mother, but his voice had changed to the plaintive call of a dove, and the only sound he was able to make was, "Hoo, hoo!"

"You are now the dove," said the manito, "and you will be a dove as long as you live. Of all birds you will be the shyest. And every one who sees you and hears your call will know that you were once afraid of Hoots, the bear."

So, for years and years, the dove flew fearfully here and there, uttering his timid call, "Hoo, hoo." At last white men came, and were sorry for him, and built dove-cotes where he and all his family could be sheltered and live in peace. There seemed to be no work at first for the doves to do, but at last it was discovered that they could carry letters tied about their necks and hidden in their feathers. They flew quickly with them to escape danger.

That is why there are pictures of doves on our valentines. The doves grew brave enough to carry messages of love from one person to another, but they are always timid and keep the love that is in the valentine a secret from all except the person to whom it is sent.

EASTER

MOLLY'S EASTER HEN

When Molly came in from the chicken house, she looked very sad.

"O dear me!" she sighed. "I'm so disappointed!"

"What is it, sunny girl?" asked mother.

"Red Top hasn't laid an egg, and to-morrow is Easter. I shut Red Top in all by herself, so I should know that it was her very own egg, and she hasn't laid any."

"But the other hens have. We shall have plenty of Easter eggs to color," said mother.

"But I was going to take one of Red Top's eggs to Auntie Brooke for Easter," said Molly, dismally.

"Wouldn't any other egg do?" asked mother.

"It wouldn't be half so nice," replied Molly. "Auntie Brooke gave me Red Top, and this is the first Easter since I had her. I told Auntie Brooke I was going to bring her one of Red Top's eggs for Easter."

"You shouldn't count on Easter eggs before they are laid," said her mother. "I am sure Auntie Brooke will understand if you take her another egg. You may color it pink, and I will let you have some gilding, so that you can mark her name on it. It will be a beautiful Easter egg."

Molly tried to smile. All day she kept going out to where Red Top was, to see whether the expected egg had been laid. That, and the work of coloring eggs for the family, kept her busy all the day. The pink eggs were beautifully colored, but she would not gild Auntie Brooke's name on one.

"I have a plan," she said. "I believe I'll have an Easter egg for Auntie Brooke, after all, mother."

On Easter morning Molly ran out into the hen-house before any one else was awake. After breakfast she slipped away; she carried a covered basket and walked very fast. First she went through the green lane that led from their house to the road, and then along the road until she came to Auntie

Brooke's. The lane was all trimmed with beautiful spring flowers for Easter, and the trees beside the road were full of birds, all singing Easter songs.

She went through Auntie Brooke's squeaky gate and along the gravel path to the side door. An old lady with a sweet face sat out on the doorstep.

"Auntie Brooke," said Molly, a little out of breath, "I've brought you an Easter egg, only it isn't laid yet. You may keep Red Top until shelays it, and then you can give her back. You'll have to excuse there not being any pink on it and your name in gilt letters, but Red Top didn't lay it in time for that."

"Thank you, dear," said Auntie Brooke, trying not to laugh. "I'm sure I shall like it just as well as if it were pink with gold letters on it."

THE SONG OF THE SPRING

The King was very ill indeed and no one in all the court could find out what was his ailment or how to cure it. He had been the kindest, merriest king for miles about, always ready to help a poor subject or to stop and play with the children as he drove his chariot through the village. Now he never smiled and he seemed too weary to care what happened in the kingdom; so everything went at sixes and sevens and no one knew what to do about it.

"The King needs daintier food," said the Court Cook, so he served broiled peacock on toast, and pomegranates and cream, and wild honey, and cheese-cakes as light as feathers, and a sponge cake made with the eggs of a bantam hen. But the King would eat none of them.

"The King needs medicine," said the Court Physician, so he searched the countryside for growing things and he brewed rose-leaf tea, and he made a potion of everlasting flowers mixed with rosemary, and he distilled wild honeysuckle with dew gathered at sunrise, but the King would drink none of these.

"Perhaps music would divert the King," suggested the Court Wise Man. "It might make him forget whatever is troubling him." And as music was the only remedy for the King's most sorrowful illness that had not been tried, the Court Herald hastened through the streets, calling as loudly as he could:

"Music for the King! Music for the King! Riches and honor for whoever can play the prettiest tune and the one that will make his majesty forget his sorrow."

Immediately the palace was filled with music, some of it very beautiful and all of it played by very famous people. A sweet singer came with his lute and sang to the King of all the princesses and queens that had listened to his tunes. But at the end the King was still weak and sorrowful. A harpist from a far country came and played music that sounded like the mighty wind on high mountain tops and the rushing flow of great mountain streams. But the King only thanked the harpist and requested that he be paid for his pains and his journey and go back to his home. Later, there came a trumpeter who gave great battle calls on his trumpet, but the King covered his ears to shut out the sound and looked more sad than ever because the sound of the trumpet gave him a headache.

So it seemed as if not even music would make the King well, and no one knew what to do.

Gladheart was the little boy who tended sheep in the valley. He was the youngest of five brothers, and there was little room and less food for them in their father's house. But Gladheart had been given his name because he always smiled over a crust of bread, even when he was a baby. Now that he was a little lad of ten with a great flock of ewes and lambs to tend and drive through sun and storm, he had smiles and kind words for all, and he played his fiddle all day long until its sweet tunes filled the valley.

"I must go and play before the King," Gladheart said one day.

"They will only laugh at your small fiddle," said his brothers, but the eldest said he would tend the sheep for a day, and Gladheart set out for the palace.

"The King will have naught to do with a shepherd lad dressed in goatskin and bearing an old fiddle," the guards at the door said. But Gladheart touched the strings with the bow and such a blithe tune came forth that the guards opened the door, and Gladheart went inside to play before the King.

At first the sight of the King sitting so bent and sorrowful on the throne with a face as frowning and sad as a storm frightened Gladheart. But he took courage and stood as straight as he could in front of the throne, and began to play on the fiddle a tune that he had learned while he was in the fields with his sheep.

It was a lovable tune, like a dozen birds and a little wandering wind and the voice of a rippling brook all joined with the sounds of the little earth singers, the bees, the katydids, and the crickets. As the King listened, his bent shoulders straightened and his face became bright with smiles. He reached out his hands to Gladheart. "I heard that tune once before when I was a boy," he said. "It makes me well to hear it now. What is it about, lad?"

"It is about the spring, your majesty," said Gladheart. "It is the song that I learned from the fields when winter was over. If your majesty will come with me to my sheep pasture, you may hear it there every day."

No one could understand why the King was suddenly so well or why he went often to sit with Gladheart and the sheep, but they were all very happy over it. And they gave Gladheart the riches and the honor that they had promised whoever could heal their King.

THE EASTER STORY

It was late in the fall when Fuzzy Caterpillar gave up.

"I suppose this is the end of me," he thought in his little round head as he tried to wriggle across the road and couldn't because his back was so stiff. "Now I am an old man and I shall never see another summer. Good-bye." And Fuzzy Caterpillar rolled himself up in a gray blanket and hung himself on the end of a dried twig. "This is the last of me," he said once more as the dried little grub he now was rattled around in the cold.

All his beautiful furry coat was scattered to the winds. The path he had made in the dust grew narrower as it wound across the road. That was because Fuzzy Caterpillar had shrivelled as he crawled. Poor Fuzzy Caterpillar, who had so loved the Out-Doors!

The winter was white, and cold, and long. Then it was over, just as all winters are over at last, and Spring came. Spring came over the hills, in a pretty new green frock and with wild flowers in her hair. Sometimes she looked up at the sky, but oftener she looked down at the ground. Spring was looking for the little creatures that she loved so much; the tiny ants, the patient spiders, the cheerful beetles, and Fuzzy Caterpillar.

"Where is Fuzzy Caterpillar?" Spring wondered. She did not see him, all dried up and hanging in his gray blanket from the twig.

"Of course Fuzzy Caterpillar is here somewhere," Spring said to herself. "And wouldn't it be nice to celebrate the day he comes out with some kind of a surprise?" The more Spring thought about this, the happier she was, and the nicer she thought it would be. So she spoke to the grass about it.

"Long Green Grasses," called Spring, "I want to make Out-Doors pretty, and celebrate the day that Fuzzy Caterpillar comes out. Will you cover the ground for me?"

So the Long Green Grasses pushed their slender fingers up out of the earth and they covered the whole ground until it was bright and green again. But the Grasses looked everywhere, and they could not see Fuzzy Caterpillar.

Then Spring spoke to the trees.

"Patient Trees," called Spring, "I want to make Out-Doors pretty, and celebrate the day that Fuzzy Caterpillar comes out. Will you cover your branches with new green leaves?"

So the Patient Trees burst their hard brown buds, and they hung new green leaves upon every one of their branches. But the leaves looked everywhere, and they could not see Fuzzy Caterpillar. All they could see was a little rolled-up gray blanket hanging from a twig.

But Spring was not one bit discouraged, and she spoke to the Laughing Brook.

"Laughing Brook," called Spring, "I want to make Out-Doors pretty, and celebrate the day that Fuzzy Caterpillar comes out. Will you run between your banks again, and sing a song?"

So the Laughing Brook began dancing and tripping over its stones again, and singing as it ran between its banks. Sometimes, though, it stopped in a quiet pool, and it could not see Fuzzy Caterpillar anywhere along its edge.

But Spring, who is very wise, was not discouraged yet, and so she spoke to the flowers.

"Sleepy Roots," called Spring, "I want to make Out-Doors pretty, and celebrate the day that Fuzzy Caterpillar comes out. Will you grow and send up plants that will bud and bloom?"

So the Sleepy Roots did just as Spring had asked them. They awoke, and they sent up leaves and buds through the earth, and the buds blossomed. So there were crocuses in purple petticoats, and daffodils in bonnets with yellow ruffles. There were tulips, red, yellow, pink, and white. They filled all the gardens, making them beautiful. And the fields were golden in the sunshine because the dandelions had bloomed again. But the flowers could not see Fuzzy Caterpillar anywhere.

Then Spring stood on the top of the hill and she looked all over the wide Out-Doors. It was very, very pretty again, so she decided that the day had come when she would celebrate.

"This is Easter Day," said Spring.

"But where is Fuzzy Caterpillar?" whispered the Long Green Grasses.

"Where is Fuzzy Caterpillar?" rustled the New Green Leaves.

"Where is Fuzzy Caterpillar?" tinkled the Brook so sadly that it did not sound like singing.

"Where is Fuzzy Caterpillar?" the wind sighed as it blew through the flowers.

Just then a wonderful thing happened. As if it had floated down from the sky, a beautiful moth flew and lighted on the tip of Spring's finger. It had all the colors of Easter in its wings, the green of the grass and the leaves, the blue of the waters, and the gold of the spring flowers. It was such a beautiful creature that only to look at it made one feel happy. But every one wondered about the moth.

"It is a stranger from far away," they said.

"Oh, no," said Spring. "Fuzzy Caterpillar has come out."

And this was true, for the gray blanket that hung from the twig was torn and empty.

BIRDS

THE BIRD

It was Serozha's birthday, and he received many different gifts; peg tops, and hobby horses, and pictures. But Serozha's uncle gave him a gift that he prized above all the rest; it was a trap for snaring birds.

The trap was constructed in such a way that a board was fitted on the frame and shut down upon the top. If seed was scattered on the board, and the trap was put out in the yard, the little bird would fly down, hop upon the board, the board would give way, and the trap would shut with a clap.

Serozha was delighted, and he ran into the house to show his mother the trap.

His mother said:

"It is not a good plaything. What do you want to do with birds? Why do you want to torture them?"

"I am going to put them in a cage," Serozha said. "They will sing, and I will feed them."

He got some seed, scattered it on the board, and set the trap in the garden. And he stood by and expected the birds to fly down. But the birds were afraid of him and would not come near the cage. Serozha ran in to get something to eat, and left the cage.

After dinner he went to look at it. The cage had shut, and in it a little bird was beating against the bars.

Serozha took up the bird, and carried it into the house.

"Mother, I have caught a bird!" he cried. "I think it is a nightingale; and how its heart beats!"

His mother said it was a wild canary. "Be careful! Don't hurt it; you would better let it go."

"No," he said. "I am going to give it something to eat and drink."

Serozha put the bird in a cage, and for two days gave it seed and water, and cleaned the cage. But on the third day he forgot all about it, and did not change the water.

And his mother said, "See here, you have forgotten your bird. You would better let it go."

Serozha thrust his hand in the cage and began to clean it, but the little bird was frightened and fluttered. After Serozha had cleaned the cage, he went to get some water. His mother saw that he had forgotten to shut the cage door, and she called after him.

"Serozha, shut up your cage, else your bird will fly out and hurt itself."

She had hardly spoken the words when the bird found the door, was delighted, spread its wings, and flew around the room toward the window. Serozha came running in, picked up the bird, and put it back in the cage. The bird was still alive, but it lay on its breast, with its wings spread out, and breathed heavily. Serozha looked and looked at it, and began to cry.

"Mother, what can I do now?" he asked.

"You can do nothing now," she replied.

Serozha stayed by the cage all day. He did nothing but look at the bird. And all the time the bird lay on its breast and breathed hard and fast.

When Serozha went to bed, the bird was dead. Serozha could not get to sleep for a long time; every time that he shut his eyes he seemed to see the bird still lying and sighing.

In the morning when Serozha went to his cage, he saw the bird lying on its back, with its legs crossed, and all stiff.

After that Serozha never again snared birds.

THE NIGHTINGALE

The Emperor's palace was the most beautiful in the world.

In the garden were to be seen wonderful flowers, and to the costliest of these silver bells were tied, which rang, so that nobody should pass by without noticing the garden. It extended so far that the gardener himself did not know where the end was. If one went on and on, one came to a glorious forest. The wood extended straight down to the sea, and in the trees lived a Nightingale. It sang so splendidly that even the poor fisherman, who had many other things to do, stopped still and listened, when he had gone out at night to throw his nets, to hear the Nightingale.

From all the countries of the world travellers came to admire the Emperor's palace and his garden, but when they heard the Nightingale they said, "That is the best of all!"

At last their words came to the Emperor.

"What's that?" he exclaimed. "I don't know the Nightingale at all. Is there such a bird in my empire, and even in my garden? I've never heard of that. I command that he shall appear this evening and sing before me!"

But where was the Nightingale to be found? The court had not heard of it either. There was a great inquiry after the wonderful Nightingale which all the world knew except the people at the palace. At last they met a poor little girl in the kitchen who said,

"Yes, I know the Nightingale well. It can sing gloriously. Every evening I get leave to carry my mother the scraps from the table. She lives down by the stream, and when I get back, and am tired, and rest in the wood, then I hear the Nightingale sing. It is just as if my mother kissed me."

So the little girl led the way out into the wood. Half the court went, and the child pointed at last to a little gray bird up in the boughs.

"It can't be possible," they said. "How dull it looks; but it may have lost its color at seeing such grand people around."

"Little Nightingale," called the kitchen maid, "our gracious Emperor wishes you to sing before him."

"My song sounds best in the greenwood," replied the Nightingale; still it came willingly when it knew what the Emperor wished.

The palace was festively adorned for it. The walls and the flooring, which were of porcelain, gleamed in the rays of thousands of golden lamps. The most glorious flowers, which could ring clearly, had been placed in all the passages. In the great hall there had been placed a golden perch on which the Nightingale sat. The little kitchen girl had received permission to stand by the door. All the court was in full dress, and all looked at the little gray bird to which the Emperor nodded.

Then the Nightingale sang so gloriously that the tears came into the Emperor's eyes, and the song went straight to his heart.

It was to remain at the palace now, the Emperor decided; to have its own cage, with liberty to go out twice every day and once at night. Twelve servants were appointed when the Nightingale went out, each of whom had a silken string fastened to the bird's leg which he held very tightly. There was really no pleasure in an excursion of that kind. The whole city spoke of the wonderful bird. When two people met, one said "Nightin," and the other said "gale" which was all that was necessary. Eleven peddlers' children were named after the bird, but not one of them could sing a note.

One day the Emperor received a large parcel, marked "The Nightingale."

He thought it was a present for the bird but when he opened it, he found a box. Inside the box was an artificial nightingale, brilliantly ornamented with diamonds, rubies, and sapphires. As soon as this artificial bird was wound up, its tail moved up and down, and shone with silver and gold. It sang very well, too, in its own way. Three and thirty times over did it sing the same waltz, and yet was not tired. The Emperor said that the living Nightingale ought to be shown this wonder.

But where was it?

None had noticed that it had flown away out of the open window, and back to the greenwood.

"What does it matter? We have the best bird after all," every one said. And the artificial bird was made to sing again and again until every one knew its tunes by heart. They liked to look at it, shining like bracelets and breastpins. The real Nightingale was banished from the empire. The artificial bird had its place on a silk cushion close to the Emperor's bed.

All the presents it received, gold and precious stones, were ranged about it. It had a title, High Imperial After-Dinner-Singer. It was certainly famous.

So a whole year went by, and then five years. The Emperor was ill and could not, it was said, live much longer. He lay on his gorgeous bed with long velvet cushions and heavy gold tassels. High up a window stood open, and the moon shone in upon the Emperor and the artificial bird.

The Emperor could scarcely breathe. It was just as if something lay upon his heart. He opened his eyes and then he saw that it was Death who sat upon his heart, and had put on his golden crown and held the Emperor's sword. And all around, from among the folds of the splendid curtains, strange heads peered forth, some ugly, and some quite lovely and mild. They were the Emperor's bad and good deeds that stood before him, now that Death sat upon his heart.

"Music! Music!" cried the Emperor, "so that I need not hear what they say! You little precious golden bird, sing, sing!"

But the bird stood still. It was worn out inside, and there was no music left in it. And Death sat and looked at the Emperor, and it was fearfully quiet.

Then there sounded from the window, suddenly, the most lovely song. It was the little live Nightingale that sat outside on a spray. It had heard of the Emperor's sad plight and had come to sing to him of comfort and hope. And as it sang the blood ran quicker and more quickly through the Emperor's heart; and even Death listened.

The Nightingale sang on and on; and it sang of the quiet churchyard where white roses grow, and the elder-blossom smells sweet, and the grass is green. Then Death felt a great longing to see his garden and he floated out at the window in a white mist, and with him went the spectres.

"Thanks! Thanks!" said the Emperor. "How can I reward you? You must always stay with me."

"Not so," replied the Nightingale. "I cannot build my nest in a palace, but I will come and sit in the evening on the spray yonder by the window and sing you something so that you may be glad and thoughtful at once. I will sing of those who are happy and those who suffer. I will sing of good and of evil that are hidden from you. The little singing bird flies far around, to the poor fishermen, to the peasant's roof, to every one who dwells far from your court. I will come and sing to you. But one thing you must promise me."

"Everything!" said the Emperor; and he stood there in his imperial robes, which he had put on himself, and pressed his sword to his heart.

"One thing, only, I beg of you," said the Nightingale, "tell no one that you have a little bird who tells you everything. Then it will go all the better."

And the Nightingale flew away.

The servants came in to look at their dead Emperor, and, yes, there he stood; and the Emperor said, "Good morning!"

HOW THE WREN BECAME KING

A long while ago when there were not so many people on the earth as there are now, and the birds and animals had things about their own way, a Cuckoo gave a tea party.

She invited all the birds there were, from the great Eagle, through the Larks, Swallows, Finches, and Crows, down to the little brown bird that sings alone in the hedges and had no name then. She seated them all around her table, although it was a task to find places for them all; and she gave each bird whatever it liked best of all to eat.

Every one wondered why the Cuckoo took such trouble as this, and certain people say to this day, "as silly as a Cuckoo," because of it; but when all the birds had eaten their fill, the Cuckoo hopped upon the table and addressed the assembled company.

"It seems to me," said the Cuckoo, "that things have been going very badly with us for some time, and that all would be remedied if we had a king to settle our affairs and rule over us. I would suggest that we choose a king to-day."

Oh, how the birds chirped, and chattered, and peeped at that. The Cuckoo had imagined that she would have the say as to which bird should be king, and she had in mind one of her own sons, but, no indeed! Each bird at the tea party was sure that he had royal blood in his veins, and they all began to argue and quarrel about it.

About that time a Rooster and a Hen passed by, taking their daily airing. They had not been invited to the tea party and so they were greatly excited at hearing the commotion; grandfathers, and fathers, and cousins, and sons among the birds were all talking and arguing at once.

"Wat? Wat?" clucked the Hen.

"I will go and see, my dear," said the Rooster, and so he rushed into the midst of the tea party to see what all the hubbub was about. When he found out, he had a plan to offer. He was often called upon to settle disputes among the Hens, so he was always quite willing to help in any such matters.

"Have a test! Have a test!" said the Rooster. "You will never decide anything by arguing in this way; but it shall be decided that the bird who is able to fly the highest shall be your king."

This seemed a fair way of settling the matter. All the birds agreed to it except the Plover, who went off into the woods and has lived there, wild, ever since.

Then the birds lighted in a row, and spread their wings, and flew with all their strength, and as high as they could, up, up into the air. One by one, though, they dropped back for they did not all have the same strength of wing. The Lark flew higher, indeed, than most of them, but finally he, too, was outstripped by the Eagle, who soared and soared until he was only a speck in the sky.

"The Eagle is our king! The Eagle is king of the birds!" sang all the others; but, no! Way, way above the Eagle flew another bird, so tiny that he looked like nothing but a mote, floating in the sunlight. It was the little brown bird that sings alone in the hedges, and had no name then. He had hidden himself in the Eagle's feathers and had been carried up with him until he wanted to fly on by himself.

"I am the king of the birds!" he twittered as he flew down among the others again.

But the other birds did not wish this. They did not like to think of so tiny and humble a bird being exalted to be their king. They were about to fall upon the little brown bird and drive him out of their midst when the Rooster spoke to them again. Since the plan had been his, he wanted to make a success of it, so he said,

"The mistake was mine, all mine. This is how we will arrange it. The bird that is able to fall deepest into the earth shall be your king."

The Rooster had a plan of his own in mind when he said this. As all the birds began to look about for places to jump into deeper places, and the Duck tried to see how long he could hold his head under water, the Rooster called to the Hen. He instructed the Hen to scratch, and when she had made a deep hole, he hid himself in it.

"I am king of the birds! I am your king!" the Rooster crowed, poking his head up out of the hole.

But the little brown bird that sings in the hedges, and had no name then, had again got the best of them all. What had he done but creep into a mouse hole, and there he was, deeper down in the earth than any of them.

"I am your king!" he twittered up to them.

Then all the birds were very much put out, for they saw that the little brown bird was truly the king. They decided, though, that they would not recognize him, and they appointed the Owl to sit, night and day, at the opening of the mouse hole and not allow the little brown bird to come out. Then all the birds went home from the Cuckoo's tea party, and to bed, for they were quite worn out with all the excitement.

All went well that night with the Owl. He watched the mouse hole and did not allow the little brown bird to so much as put his bill out. When it came to be day, though, the Owl was tired, and he closed, first, one eye, and then the other eye. There he was, fast asleep, and out hopped the little brown bird who had a name now, because he was the little Hedge King.

It was a great disappointment to the other birds to be obliged to recognize so humble a little brown bird as their king, and they blamed the Owl for it. That is why he still sleeps in the daytime now, and looks about only at night. And that is why, also, he is such an enemy of the mice, continually hunting them in their holes.

But the little brown bird who sings alone in the hedges really made himself king of the birds. He has two names now, Hedge King, and Wren.

SUMMER

THE LITTLE RED PRINCESS

Every one knew that she was a princess because she wandered all day through the castle without doing any work. It was a very busy kingdom indeed even if it was so tiny. It was only about two inches high above the meadow, not nearly as tall as the grass blades that grew all around it. The grass looked like a forest of trees to the little red princess, and a wild forget-me-not that bent down over the castle made her sky, for it was almost as blue and nearly as large to her wee eyes.

There were many roads and streets that went up and down through the kingdom, none of them much wider than the stalk of a daisy. There were many little houses along the streets and there was the castle of the little red princess with more windows than one could count, and more winding passages than she could walk through.

The castle was full of other busy little people in red who waited on the princess. They milked her cows, and played with her, and managed the house-keeping so that she did not have to do a bit of work. She was the only one, though, in the whole kingdom who did not work.

As the little red princess looked from her highest window she saw her subjects hurrying to and fro. They were always bringing sand for building, whole lines of them, and putting up new houses, and making better roads. Sentinels watched the gates of the city, and hundreds of workers in red brought in food from the meadow.

If one could have heard so tiny a person as the little red princess speak, she would have said,

"Why should I work when I have so many subjects to wait upon me? I was intended to look pretty, and sit in my doorway, and keep the whole kingdom working for me!"

One day something wonderful happened. The little red princess felt a strange pricking on her shoulders. When she turned her tiny head about to see what was the matter, she found out that she had a beautiful pair of wee, gossamer wings!

If any of the little red workers of the kingdom had been in doubt as to whether their princess were a real princess or not, they were sure now. Hadn't she wings? They waited on the princess more carefully than ever for fear she might hurt herself. And they declared a holiday for her to try her wings when they would stop work and go with her outside of the kingdom.

The little red princess was very much excited indeed about her flight. She had never been outside in all her life, and she went at the head of a procession, all the workers dancing and running along beside her.

Oh, how wonderful she found it in the meadow! The wind in the grass was like a forest wind to her. The sun dazzled her. Now she knew that the blue flower was not at the top of things. Far, far above it was more blue, and yellow sunlight, that she thought was gold, shone all for her because she was a princess!

She spread her wings! Up, up she flew! The others who had no wings watched her and clapped their hands as she rose in the bright air. It was not such a very long flight, not much higher than a tall parasol of Queen Anne's lace, but it was like flying into the clouds to the little red princess.

"I shall fly all the time!" she thought to herself. "I will alight only long enough to tell my subjects to go back to work for me. I am going to fly all the rest of the time."

So the little red princess dropped lightly to the ground again.

How they crowded about her! But she pushed them all aside a little scornfully. They looked surprised and tried to lead her toward the gate of the kingdom again. Then she pushed harder, and stamped her tiny feet. She tried to spread her wings, but they would not let her.

The little red workers surrounded their princess. They began cutting off her wings! It was a rule of the kingdom that a princess might fly only once. She did not know it, of course.

Some princesses were satisfied with trying their wings just once and then took them off themselves, but she was not that kind of princess. She wanted wings all the time!

She struggled, and tried to bite her kind little red subjects who really knew what was best for her. They did not pay any attention to her, though. They did not hurt her very much, but they did not stop until every scrap of her gossamer wings was gone.

"Now look at me! Just see what you have done to your princess!" she tried to say.

"Yes, just look! See what has happened to you!" the others tried to reply, hopping merrily around her.

It was true. Something wonderful had happened to the little red princess. She had changed into a little red queen!

So she did not mind in the least losing her wings. In fact, she was rather glad. She went home to the castle and went right to work ordering her servants about, and keeping house, and taking care of her royal family and all the nurses. She very seldom has time to look out of her castle window, so you may never see her. Her kingdom lies very near you, though, for the little red queen is the real, true queen of the ant hill!

HOW THE FLOWERS CAME

Ever so many years ago the world was as bare and gray as the roads. The Earth King grew very tired of it, and covered the ground with a carpet of green. We call it grass. For years and years there was nothing but green, until the Earth King grew as tired of the green as he had been of the gray. He decided that he must have more colors. So one day he took his royal retinue and journeyed to a hillside where he knew there grew the finest grasses in all the kingdom. At the blast of the King's bugler the grasses assembled, and the King addressed them in simple words.

"My faithful grasses," he said. "It is many years since I placed you here. You have served me well. You have kept true green. It now pleases me to announce to you that I am about to reward a certain number of you and make you lords and ladies of the field. To-morrow I shall come hither at this same hour. You are to assemble before me, and the fairest of your number and the most pleasing I will honor with a great and lasting reward. Farewell."

How the grasses whispered and put their heads together then as a breeze crept up the hillside! They arose next morning before the sun, that they might wash their ribbons in the gleaming pearls of dew. What prinking and preening! What rustling of ruffles and sashes! What burnishing of armor and spears! At length the King's bugle rang out to call them into grand assembly. Full of excitement, they stood before the King, each hoping that he might be chosen for one of the great honors.

The King greeted them as he had on the previous day, but he said,

"In this Court of Judgment I must have willing servants to help me. First, I must have a keeper of the gate so that no outsider may enter. Which one of this host will be keeper of the gate?"

Not a man-grass stirred in his tracks, for each feared that if he became a servant of the King he would lose his chance to be a lord.

"Which one?" asked the King again. "Which one will volunteer to keep the gate for me?"

At this moment a sturdy grass was seen coming down the hillside. He was not handsome, but he was strong. His shoulders were broad, and his chest was deep, and he was armed to the teeth. Spear points stuck from every one of his pockets, and in each hand he carried a lance as sharp as lightning.

"Let the others wait for their honors," he thought, as he said,

"I will serve the King."

"So be it," said the King. "Take your station at the gate. And now," continued the King, "I must have a herald to announce my awards and my commands. Who will be my herald?"

Again there was silence among the man-grasses, until at last one was seen to advance. He was short and round and smiling, as happy a grass as grew on the hill. He came before the King as fast as his short legs could carry him.

"So it please the King," he said. "I will be his royal herald."

"So be it," said the King. "Stand here at my feet."

"Two torch-bearers I need," the King went on, "two torch-bearers, tall and comely, to hold the lights on high. Who will serve the King as torch-bearers?"

And now there was silence and stiffness among the lady-grasses as each feared to lose her chance to be given a title, and waited for the others. At last two slender grass-maidens advanced with glowing faces but reluctant step. They were not as beautiful as some of their sisters. Their ribbons were few and some of them were frayed. They scarcely expected the King to accept them, but they meekly offered themselves, as they said,

"We, O King, will be your torch-bearers."

The King looked greatly pleased as he replied,

"So be it, indeed. Stand here on either hand. And now," continued the King, "I must have an incense-bearer to swing my censer over the meadows. Who will be my incense-bearer?"

For a moment there was silence again among the lady-grasses, but only for a moment. Then out stepped one of the daintiest of them all. She tripped quickly and quietly down the hill to the King, saying modestly as she approached,

"I will be your incense-bearer."

"Let it be so," said the King. "Await my commands. Yet one more servant," he added. "I need some one to ring the chimes. Who among all these loyal subjects, man or maid, will ring the chimes?"

Scarcely had the King's words left his lips when one of the noblest grasses of all, her broad green ribbons rustling as she moved, left the crowded ranks of the grasses, and eagerly advanced before the King. "If it please your Majesty, I will ring the chimes," she said.

Then the King looked around, satisfied, upon his eager and expectant audience, and spoke a few brief words to them. He had come, he said, fearing that the task was almost too great for even a king—to choose among so many and so beautiful subjects. But they had helped him by choosing for themselves, and he had now only to award the honors.

"Keeper of the gate," he commanded, "stand before the King!"

The keeper of the gate came awkwardly forward, pricking all who brushed against him as he passed.

"Because you have been willing to serve," said the King, "I reward you with distinguished honor." Then, taking from the hand of a page a great velvet cap of purplish red, he placed it upon the head of the gatekeeper, saying as he did so, "I dub you: My Lord, the Thistle.

"Let the King's herald stand forth!"

The little round, happy herald obeyed. The King took a great gold coronet from the hand of a page and placed it upon the herald's head, saying,

"Because of your readiness to serve the King, I create you a noble of the field, and dub you: My Lord, the Dandelion.

"Let the torch-bearers stand forth!"

Then the two shy grass-maidens bowed before the King. On the head of each the King placed a shining crown, one all gold, and the other of gold rimmed with white, that they might be told apart; and he said to them,

"Because of your generous deed, I dub you: Lady Buttercup and Lady Daisy.

"Now, my incense-bearer!"

The dainty grass-maiden knelt at his feet and bowed her head.

The King beckoned to a page, who brought him a tiny hood of beautiful blue. This the King placed upon her head, saying,

"I am grateful for your service. I dub you: Lady Violet.

"Let the ringer of the royal chimes appear!"

The beautiful grass with the broad, shining ribbons stood proudly before him, and bent her head in salute. The King took a silver bell and gave it to her, saying,

"This shall be the sign of your royal office. I dub you: Lady Lily-of-the-Field."

Then the King charged his new-made lords and ladies to be faithful to their service, and never cease, year by year, to return and beautify the earth. Then the assembly was dissolved, but not until the whole host of grasses on the hillside had applauded what the King had done. They were disappointed, but they knew that the bravest and truest had been made the most beautiful among them, and crowned with the honor due.

THE THREE LITTLE BUTTERFLY BROTHERS

There were once three little butterfly brothers, one white, one red, and one yellow. They played in the sunshine, and danced among the flowers in the garden, and they never grew tired because they were so happy.

One day there came a heavy rain and it wet their wings. They flew away home, but when they got there they found the door locked and the key gone. So they had to stay outdoors in the rain, and they grew wetter and wetter.

By and by they flew to the red and yellow striped tulip, and said, "Friend Tulip, will you open your flower-cup and let us in until the storm is over."

The tulip answered: "The red and yellow butterflies may enter because they are like me, but the white one may not come in."

But the red and yellow butterflies said: "If our white brother may not find shelter in your flower-cup, why, then, we will stay outside in the rain with him."

It rained harder and harder, and the poor little butterflies grew wetter and wetter, so they flew to the white lily and said: "Good Lily, will you open your bud a little so we may creep in out of the rain?"

The lily answered, "The white butterfly may come in, because he is like me, but the red and yellow ones must stay outside in the storm."

Then the white butterfly said: "If you won't receive my red and yellow brothers, why, then, I will stay out in the rain with them. We would rather be wet than parted."

So the three little butterflies flew away.

But the sun, who was behind a cloud, heard it all. He knew what good little brothers the butterflies were and how they had kept together in spite of the wet. So the sun pushed his face through the clouds and chased away the rain, and shone brightly on the garden.

He dried the wings of the three little butterflies, and warmed their bodies. They ceased to sorrow, and danced among the flowers until evening. Then they flew away home, and found the door wide open.

ANIMALS

WHY PETER RABBIT WEARS A WHITE PATCH

The Merry Little Breezes of Old Mother West Wind had been tumbled out of her big bag very early one morning. Indeed, they were hardly awake when Old Mother West Wind shook them out on the Green Meadows and hurried away to her day's work, for she knew it was to be a very busy day.

The Merry Little Breezes had watched her go. They saw the great windmill in Farmer Brown's barn-yard begin to whirl as she passed. They saw the million little leaves of the Green Forest shake, until a million little drops of dew, like a million little diamonds, fell down to the earth. And then Old Mother West Wind disappeared on her way to the Great Ocean, there to blow the white-winged ships along their way all day long.

The Merry Little Breezes stretched themselves and then began to dance across the Great Meadows to kiss the buttercups and daisies and to waken the sleepy little meadow people, who hadn't got their nightcaps off yet. But no one wanted to play so early in the morning. No, Sir, no one wanted to play. You see every one had something more important to do. They loved the Merry Little Breezes, but they just couldn't stop to play. Finally the Merry Little Breezes gave it up and just curled up among the grasses for a sun-nap. That is, all but one did. That one kept hopping up every few minutes to see if any one was in sight who would be likely to play a little while.

By and by he saw Peter Rabbit coming down the Lone Little Path from the Green Forest on his way to the dear old briar-patch on the Green Meadows. Peter looked sleepy. The truth is, Peter had been out all night, and he was on his way home.

Half-way down the Lone Little Path Peter stopped, and sitting up very straight, looked over towards the Smiling Pool. He could see Mr. Redwing flying 'round and 'round, this way and that way over the bulrushes. He could hear Mr. Redwing's voice, and it sounded as if Mr. Redwing was very much excited. The more Mr. Peter looked and listened, the more certain he became that something very important must have happened over in the bulrushes on the edge of the Smiling Pool.

Now curiosity is Peter Rabbit's besetting sin. Sleepy as he was, he just couldn't go home without first finding out what had happened in the bulrushes. So away Peter started for the Smiling Pool, lipperty-lipperty-lip. Of course the Merry Little Breeze saw him go. Then the Merry Little Breeze waked all the other Merry Little Breezes, and away they all danced across the Green Meadows to the Smiling Pool and stole in among the bulrushes behind Peter Rabbit to see what he was about. They came up just in time to hear Peter say:

"Hello, Mr. Redwing! You seem very much excited this fine morning. What is it all about? Has anything happened?"

Mr. Redwing hovered right over Peter Rabbit.

"Tra-la-la-la-lee, cherokee, cherokee!I'm happy, oh, so happy! I am happy as can be!"

sang Mr. Redwing, looking down at Peter, who was sitting very straight and looking up.

"You seem to be. But what is it all about? What is it that makes you so happy this morning, Mr. Redwing?" Peter asked.

"Tra-la-la-la-lee, cherokee, cherokee!We've another speckled egg, and this one makes it three!"

carolled Mr. Redwing, and flew over to the nest in the bulrushes where Mrs. Redwing was fussing about in a very important manner.

"Pooh!" said Peter Rabbit. "Is that all? What a little thing to make such a fuss about. I think I'll pay my respects to Grandfather Frog and then I'll go home."

Peter yawned. Then he hopped out where he could see all over the Smiling Pool. There sat Grandfather Frog on his big green lily-pad, just as usual.

"Good morning, Grandfather Frog!" said Peter Rabbit.

"Chugarum! Of course it's good morning. Every morning is good," replied Grandfather Frog gruffly.

"Oh!" said Peter Rabbit, and then he couldn't think of another thing to say.

The Merry Little Breezes giggled, and Grandfather Frog looked over at them and very slowly winked. Then he rolled his big goggly eyes up and stared into the sky. Peter Rabbit looked up to see what Grandfather Frog was looking at so intently. There was Redtail the Hawk swinging 'round and 'round in great big circles, as if he were trying to bore his way right into the clouds. Peter didn't stop to watch.

"When ol' Mr. Hawk is a-riding in the sky,Keep a-moving, keep a-moving, keep a-moving mighty spry!"

chanted Peter, and taking his own advice, off he went, lipperty-lipperty-lip.

Grandfather Frog watched the white patch of the seat of Peter's pants bobbing through the rushes until finally Peter was out of sight.

"Did you ever hear how Peter Rabbit happens to always wear a white patch on the seat of his pants?" asked Grandfather Frog.

"No; do tell us," exclaimed the Merry Little Breezes of Old Mother West Wind.

Grandfather Frog snapped up a foolish green fly, smacked his lips, cleared his throat, and began:

"Once upon a time when the world was young, Old Mother Nature found she had her hands full. Yes, Sir, she certainly did have her hands full. Her family was so big that she couldn't keep an eye on each one all the time. Dear me, dear me, such a lot of trouble as Old Mother Nature did have in those days! And no one made her more trouble than Peter Rabbit's grandfather a thousand times removed. Mr. Rabbit was always in mischief. He just naturally couldn't keep out of it. He just hopped out of one scrape right plumb into another.

"Seemed like Old Mother Nature was busy just straightening out trouble Mr. Rabbit had made. Even she wasn't always quite sure who had made it, and no one else suspected Mr. Rabbit at all. He wore a brown coat, just like the brown leaves, and when he ran he looked just like a little old bunch of leaves blowing along. So Mr. Rabbit used to creep up and listen to what others were saying, for he was just as curious as Peter Rabbit is now, and he used to play all kinds of tricks and never get caught, because of that little old brown suit of his.

"One day in the early spring, when gentle Sister South Wind had melted all the snow, excepting a little patch right under the window of Mr. Skunk's house, Mr. Rabbit came strolling along that way with nothing special on his mind. Mr. and Mrs. Skunk were having a little family talk, and Mr. Skunk was speaking some loud. Mr. Rabbit stopped. Then Mr. Rabbit grinned and sat right down on that bed of snow under Mr. Skunk's window, where he could hear every word.

"Mr. Rabbit had been a-sitting there some time, listening to things that were none of his business, when he happened to look up. There was Old Mother Nature coming through the woods. She hadn't seen him yet, and Mr. Rabbit didn't mean that she should. Off he ran as fast as he could through the brown leaves, chuckling to himself. But Mr. Rabbit had forgotten to brush off the seat of his pants, and of course they were all white with snow.

"Old Mother Nature's eyes are sharp, and so of course she saw the white spot bobbing through the bushes, saw it right away. Mr. Rabbit had to stop and tell what he had been doing to get the seat of his pants all white with snow, and he told the truth, for it's of no use to tell anything else to Old Mother Nature. She looked very stern and she opened her mouth to tell Mr. Rabbit what she thought of him, and just then she had an idea. She just marched Mr. Rabbit off and sewed a white patch on the seat of his pants. And after that, when Mr. Rabbit tried to run away from the mischief he had got into, every one knew who it was by the white patch on the seat of his pants.

"And from that day to this all of Mr. Rabbit's family have worn a white patch, and that is why Peter wears one now, and whenever he stops running, if it is only for a minute, sits down on it so that it cannot be seen," concluded Grandfather Frog.

"Thank you! Thank you, Grandfather Frog!" cried the Merry Little Breezes, and hurried to see who would be the first one to blow a big, fat, foolish green fly within reach of Grandfather Frog's mouth.

THE ANIMALS' NEW YEAR'S EVE

Centuries ago, in Sweden, a dean was riding through the dense forest on a New Year's Eve. He was on horseback, dressed in a fur coat and cap. On the pommel of his saddle hung a satchel in which he carried his book of prayers. He had been with a sick person who lived in a far away forest settlement until late in the evening. Now he was on his way home but he feared that he should not get back to his house until after midnight.

The dean's horse was strong and sturdy, and quite as wise as a human being. He could find his way home from any part of the forest. So the dean rode along now in the gray night, through the bewildering woods, with the reins dangling and his thoughts far away. It was a long time before he noticed how far along he was on his homeward way. When he did glance up, he saw that the forest was as dense as it had been at the beginning.

He intended to turn the horse at once, but the animal had never strayed. Perhaps he, himself, was mistaken, the dean thought. But suddenly a big branch struck him and almost swept him from the horse.

They were riding over a soft marsh through which there was no beaten track, although the horse trotted along at a brisk pace and showed no uncertainty. The dean seized the reins and turned the horse about, guiding him back to the roadway. No sooner was he there than he turned again and made straight for the woods.

The dean decided to walk and lead the horse until they came to more familiar roads. He dismounted, wound the reins around his arm, and started along on foot. It was no easy matter to tramp through the forest in a heavy fur coat; and the horse refused to follow. He planted his hoofs firmly on the ground and balked.

At last the dean was angry. He had never beaten his horse, nor would he now. Instead he threw the reins down and walked away.

"We may as well part company, since you want to go your own way," he said.

He had not taken more than two steps before the horse came after him, took a cautious grip on his master's coat sleeve, and stopped him. Afterward the dean could not understand how it happened but, dark as it was, the horse looked straight in his eyes. He gave his master a look that was both pleading and reproachful.

"I have served you day after day and done your bidding," he seemed to say. "Will you not follow me this one night?"

Without further delay the dean sprang into the saddle.

"Go on!" he said. "I will not desert you when you are in trouble."

He let the horse go as he wished and it was a hazardous journey, uphill all the way. The forest grew so thick that he could not see two feet ahead, but it seemed as if they were climbing a high mountain. The horse took perilous steps.

"Surely you don't intend to go up Black's Ridge, do you?" asked the dean, who knew that was one of the highest peaks in Hälsingland.

They mounted up and up, and the higher they went the more scattering were the trees. At last they rode on bare highland where the dean could look in every direction. Great tracts of land went up and down in mountains and valleys covered with dark trees. He could make out where they were.

"Why, of course it's Black's Ridge!" he said. "What an adventure!"

When they were at the top the horse stopped behind a thick pine, as if to hide. The dean bent forward and pushed aside the branches that he might see.

The mountain's bald top was there. It was not empty, though. In the middle of the open space was an immense boulder around which many wild beasts were gathered. They were having a meeting of some sort.

Near to the big rock he saw bears, so firmly and heavily built that they seemed like fur-clad figures of stone. They were lying down and their little eyes blinked impatiently, for they had come from their winter sleep to attend court and could hardly keep awake. Behind the bears, in tight rows, were hundreds of wolves. They were not sleepy, for wolves are more alert in winter than in summer. They sat upon their haunches, like dogs, whipping the ground with their tails and panting—their tongues lolling far out of their jaws.

Behind the wolves, the lynx skulked, stiff-legged and clumsy, like misshapen cats. They hissed and spat when one came near them. The row back of the lynx was filled with wolverines; they had dog faces and bear coats. They were not happy on the ground, and they stamped their pads impatiently, longing to get into the trees. Behind them, covering the entire space of the forest border, leaped the foxes, the weasels, and the martens. They were small and perfectly formed, but they looked even more savage and blood thirsty than the larger beasts.

All this the dean plainly saw for the whole place was light. Upon the huge rock at the centre was the Wood-nymph, who held in her hand a pine torch which burned in a big red flame. The Nymph was as tall as the tallest tree in the forest. She wore a spruce-brush mantle, and had spruce-cone hair. She stood very still, her face turned toward the forest. She was watching and listening.

Suddenly the dean heard the sound of a familiar bell. The next moment he heard footfalls and crackling of branches, as of many animals breaking through the forest. A big herd of cattle was climbing the mountain. They came through the forest in the order in which they had marched to the mountain ranches. First came the bell cow followed by the bull, then the other cows and the calves. After them came the goats, and last were the horses and colts. The sheep-dog trotted along beside the sheep; but neither shepherd nor shepherdess was with them.

The domestic animals came in great terror, straight toward the wild beasts. The cattle came with faltering step; the goats had no desire to play or butt. The bodies of the horses were all a-quiver with fright. The most pathetic of all was the sheep-dog. He kept his tail between his legs and crawled on the ground.

As the creatures reached the summit and filed past the Wood-nymph, the dean saw her lower her pine torch over one and another of them.

Every time this happened the wild beasts broke into exultant roars, particularly when the Wood-nymph indicated a cow or some other large creature. The animal that saw the torch turned toward it, uttered a frightful cry, as if it had received a knife thrust in its flesh. Herd upon herd followed, without a break in the line of procession. It was the same with all.

Then the dean understood the meaning of what he saw. He had heard that the animals assembled on Black's Ridge every New Year's Eve that the Wood-nymph might mark out which of the tame beasts would that year be eaten by the wild beasts. It was terrible! He thought of the farmers who had so much love for their creatures.

"They would risk their own lives rather than let their cattle be doomed by the Wood-nymph," the dean thought.

The last herd to come was the dean's own, from the rectory farm. He heard the sound of his bell cow a long way off. The horse, too, must have heard it, for he began to shake in every limb and was bathed in sweat.

"So it is your turn to pass before the Wood-nymph and receive your sentence," the dean said to the horse. "Don't be afraid. Now I know why you brought me here, and I shall not leave you."

The beautiful cattle from the rectory farm came out of the forest and marched to the Wood-nymph and the wild beasts. Last in line was the horse. The dean did not leave the saddle, but let the animal take him to the Wood-nymph.

The dean had nothing for his defence, but he had taken out his book of prayers and sat pressing it to his heart. At first he seemed unnoticed, but his cattle filed by and the Wood-nymph did not lower her pine torch toward any of these. When the faithful horse stepped forward, though, she made a movement to mark him for death.

Instantly the dean held up his book of prayers, and the torch light fell on its cover. The Wood-nymph uttered a loud, shrill cry; and the torch dropped from her hand and fell to the ground.

Immediately the flame was extinguished, and all about was the profound stillness of a wilderness in winter. Then the dark clouds parted, and through the opening stepped the full round moon to shed its light upon the ground. Not one of the many wild beasts was there. The dean and his horse were alone on Black's Ridge, the horse trembling and foaming.

By the time the dean reached home he no longer knew if it had been a vision or reality — this that he had seen; but he took it as a warning to him to remember the poor creatures who are at the mercy of wild beasts. He preached so powerfully to the peasants that in his day all the wild beasts were exterminated in that part of the country.

THE COUNTRY CAT

Cats and mice didn't use to be such bad friends as they are now. They used to visit back and forth, once upon a time, just like neighbors.

What made them fall out?

Well, it came about this way.

Old Miss Pussy Cat lived in the country but she was very curious to know about town doings. She told all her friends and relatives how she longed to see the sights.

In the middle of the night Mr. Gray Moose knocked on her door, and said that he had a cousin going up to town. If Miss Pussy Cat still wanted to see the sights this cousin would be proud to give her a lift.

Then Miss Pussy Cat tied on her bonnet, and put on her shawl, and packed a basket full of victuals, and started out with Mr. Mouse. Mice do their travelling by night, and the cat and the mouse travelled all night, and they got to town the next day.

When they came where all the people were, Mr. Mouse picked up his feet and ran down a rat hole; but Miss Pussy Cat sat down by the side of the road to eat a little. She was sitting there, spreading out all her good country sausage and good country ham and such things, when a town cat came prowling along past.

This town cat was hungry. He was just as ragged as a beggar man, and he wanted Miss Pussy Cat's victuals mighty bad.

"My land," he said. "Where did you get that big lunch?"

"Oh, that's just a little snack," said Miss Pussy Cat very politely. "I brought it with me from home. Won't you join me, sir?"

Now that old, hungry town cat wanted all Miss Pussy Cat's victuals mighty bad. He didn't want to join her. So he said, "Do you really eat such a mess as that in the country where you come from?"

"Yes, indeed," said Miss Pussy Cat, who was mighty glad to meet even a beggar cat from town and learn town ways.

"Don't you eat sausages and ham in town? What do you eat in town, anyway?" she asked.

The town cat looked all about. He was bound to send Miss Pussy Cat on an errand that would take her away from those good victuals. Just then he saw Mr. Mouse peep out of the hole to ask Miss Pussy Cat if she was having a good time. The town cat reasoned that if he could start Miss Pussy Cat running after Mr. Swift Foot Mouse he would have time to steal her dinner.

"We eat mice!" he said in the grandest manner. "You never will learn town ways until you learn to eat mice."

Miss Pussy Cat was bound she would learn to do as town folks did. Up she hopped and left the lunch as quick as you could wink—and the old, hungry town cat grabbed it just as quickly. Miss Pussy Cat chased Mr. Mouse all the way to the Court House. There she caught him and there she ate him, all but his squeak and his teeth.

Then, by that, she got the taste; and cats have been eating mice and rats ever since, to this day.

FAIRIES

THE THREE BROTHERS

Once upon a time there lived three poor little dwarfs in a tumble-down house by a roadside, and each dwarf owned a china mug.

One little dwarf was stingy. He did his mug up in tissue paper and cotton batting and kept it locked up in his third bureau drawer. "I will keep it safe," said he, "where nobody can ever use it. It is my mug. My mug shall never get broken, and when I need a mug to drink from, I can use one that belongs to some one else."

The second little dwarf was selfish. He carried his mug in his pocket. "I am going to keep this mug to drink from myself. It belongs to me. If others need a mug to drink from, let them look out for themselves," he said.

The third little dwarf was generous. "I'm so glad that I own a pretty mug!" he chuckled to himself. "Every one can use it. It is the very thing to offer a thirsty traveller who stops at our tumble-down house to ask for a drink of water. My brothers can use it, too. I am sure they will both be quite as careful of it as if it belonged to them. We need only the one mug, for we share alike, because we love one another."

Now one day there came a traveller over the dusty highroad. He was thirsty and tired. He saw the well, and he went up to the door of the tumble-down house and knocked, rat-tat-tat!

The stingy little dwarf was yawning in the parlor, because he never did any work—he let the others do it. When he heard the rat-tat-tat he kept very quiet.

The selfish little dwarf was in the dining-room, pretending to sweep—but he was only sweeping the crumbs under the mat, for he did not like to clean. He heard the rat-tat-tat! but he pretended that he was too busy to answer it.

The third little dwarf was in the kitchen, scrubbing the hearth with a mop. His sleeves were rolled up, and he had overalls on, but he could not bear to keep a tired traveller waiting at the door. "I must go at once," he thought. And he went.

"Come right round to the well," he said. "I will get a mug and give you a drink of our nice cold water. You must be tired, for the highway is warm, and dusty." He set the best chair for the traveller, and gave him a fan.

He went to fetch his mug. But what do you think! When he found it at last, it was soiled—and the stingy dwarf had carelessly broken the handle off, and the selfish dwarf had dropped it on the floor and nicked the rim! "Oh! Oh! It's not fit for company use!" cried the generous little dwarf. "I must have something better!"

He asked Stingy to let him take his mug.

"No. You can't take mine," said Stingy. "Nobody can ever use it. It is all put away. It's mine, and I won't lend it to anybody."

Then he asked Selfish to let him take his mug.

"No," said Selfish. "I can't let you take my mug. Give him yours. What do you care if it is nicked, and the handle is off—it is good enough for a beggar, I should think!"

So there was nothing for the generous little dwarf to do except to take his own broken mug to the stranger. But he cut some slices of bread and put them on the prettiest plate that he could find.

"I'm sorry I haven't a better mug to offer you," he said, "but the others were all put away. They belong to my brothers. Oh, I wish that they would come out to see you,—they are so nice,—but they said they were busy at present. Stingy is dusting the parlor, and Selfish is brushing up the dining-room. Their mugs are nicer than mine, because they always know just how to take care of their things. Wouldn't you like some more bread? I am sorry we haven't butter to offer you—but we never buy it."

The traveller thanked Generous for all he had done. He said, "I am so grateful to you that I should like to do something for you before I go. I should like to give you something to remember me by. Let me take your mug again, little dwarf. Have you a big pail that I can use?"

"Oh, yes," returned the generous little dwarf. "I have one." And he ran to the kitchen and rinsed out the one that he had been using.

The stranger took the broken mug that had lost its handle and had a chipped rim, and he began to dip water from the bucket into the pail.

At the first dip, the handle came back on the mug, and the mug became quite whole and new. At the second dip, the mop-pail turned into gold. At the third dip, the tumble-down house became new and splendid. At the fourth dip, the cupboards became filled with pots, kettles, and good things to eat. At the fifth dip, Stingy and Selfish came running out of the house, and they were changed. They were not stingy or selfish any longer, but were like their brother, generous, and good, and loving. They carried their mugs and gave them to thestranger. And they kissed the generous little brother dwarf. The one who had been stingy said he was sorry that he had never helped with the work. And the one who had been selfish said that he was sorry, too, and that he never would sweep crumbs under the mat again — for it only made work for other people to do. And at the seventh dip, the pail was filled full of gold.

Then the stranger bade them good-bye, and went on his way.

Who was he? A good fairy, no doubt. He may have heard of the generous little dwarf, and wanted to help him. If that were so, he probably wanted to help Stingy and Selfish, too, and make them into Good and Happy. At any rate, they all lived happily ever after, and the mug that belonged to the generous little dwarf was kept at the wellside for travellers to use.

THE CRY FAIRY

There was once a fairy who wanted to know all the things that ever were. This was very unusual, because most fairies know a great deal more than they have time to do; but somehow this fairy, who was named Gillibloom, had an idea that mortals know a great deal and that fairies would be happier if they could find out what some of the things are.

So he went to the Fairy Queen and asked for leave of absence for thirty-three and a third years, that he might go and live among mortals and learn things.

At the end of thirty-three and a third years he came back again, and he found the fairies dancing just as if they had never left off. They were all perfectly delighted to see him, and they left off dancing and crowded round him and cried out all together, which is the way the fairies sometimes talk: "O Gillibloom, what have you learned?"

Gillibloom looked at them a few minutes very solemnly, as if he wanted them to pay great attention to what he was going to say. Then he answered: "I have not really learned anything, but I have almost learned to cry."

"To cry, Gillibloom?" called the fairies. "What is that?"

"I know," cried a fairy who was a great traveller, and had once gone on a moonbeam excursion to a large town. "It's what mortals do when they want something they haven't got, or have something they don't want."

"Yes," said Gillibloom, "that is it."

"But what good is it?" asked the other fairies.

"I don't really know," said Gillibloom: "but I think it is really very good indeed, because so many of them do it. Sometimes if you are very little and want something, and cry and cry, somebody brings it to you."

"But we don't want anything we can't get without crying," said the fairies.

"Yes, that is true," said Gillibloom. "But it can't be that so many people would cry if there wasn't some use in it. Try as I may, I can't find out what the use is, but I thought I might form a class and we could all cry together, and then we should see what happened."

Now some of the fairies were too busy painting flowers to join a class, and more were too busy riding on bees' wings, but there were a few dozen who said:

"We might as well join. Why not? It will please Gillibloom, and maybe there is some use in it, after all."

So Gillibloom appointed the next night by the banks of the Standing Pool, for, he said, it would be quite impossible at first to cry anywhere except by the side of still water.

The next night they were all there, twenty-seven of them, each with a moss-cup in his hand.

So the fairies all sat down in a circle, and looked pleasantly about at one another and said: "We are here to cry."

"Now, in the beginning," said Gillibloom, "I will show you how it is done. The first three of you there by the acorn must run at me and knock off my cap."

So the first three ran gaily at him and knocked off his cap, but they might as well not have done it, for another cap, just as green and with just as red a feather, blew right down from somewhere else and settled on his head, and the fairies laughed, and Gillibloom did, too.

"Well," said he, "the next three of you must trip me up, and I'll fall down on the ground, and then I'll show you how to cry."

So the next three tripped him up, and Gillibloom didn't mind it in the least, because, whatever you do in the fairy woods, it never hurts. But he remembered that he was the teacher, and if he didn't begin to teach he would pretty soon be no teacher at all. So he sat there on the ground and made up a dreadful face, and wrinkled his forehead and shut his eyes and pulled down the corners of his mouth. And then he dipped his own moss-cup carefully into the Standing Pool, and brought up a drop of water. And he put his fingers in it and splashed some on his face; and it ran down his cheeks, and he said proudly: "Now I am almost crying."

"Ho!" said the fairies, "is that all? We can do that without being taught."

So they wrinkled up their foreheads and shut their eyes and drew down their mouths and dipped their fingers in the moss-cups, and sprinkled their faces, and made a bellowing noise, and they said proudly: "Now we are almost crying, too."

Gillibloom had opened his eyes and wiped his cheeks on a bit of everlasting petal.

"That was very good," he said, "very good indeed! To-morrow we will go on with the second lesson."

But the twenty-seventh fairy was thinking just then that he might have been dancing all this time, and he said: "Gillibloom, I don't see what good it will do."

"It must be remembered that we have only learned Almost Crying to-day," said Gillibloom, with dignity. "When we have learned Quite Crying it will be a different matter."

"I can't help it," said the twenty-seventh fairy. "I'm not coming any more. Anybody want my cup?"

But nobody did, because all the other pupils had kept their cups very carefully, and he tossed it into the Standing Pool and danced away through the forest, singing:

"School's dismissed! School's dismissed!Out of so many I shan't be missed.By and by they'll learn to cry.But if any one's there, it won't be I.I'd rather sing or dance or fly,Or swim in a puddle where star-shines lie.I'll not cry — not I!"

And the next day it was just the same. The twenty-six fairies, sat by the side of the Standing Pool, and Gillibloom wrinkled up his forehead and shut his eyes and drew down his mouth and bellowed and wet his cheeks with water out of his moss-cup, and they all did the same, and then they said: "Now we are Almost Crying."

But when the lesson was over, the twenty-sixth fairy said he had some wheat ripening to attend to in a field ever so far away, and the next day the twenty-fifth fairy said there was a Crow Caucus on, and he wanted to see what they meant to do about the scare-crow in the field they owned, and he couldn't come any more, and the next day the twenty-fourth fairy said there were ever so many dancing steps he hadn't practised for a long time, and he couldn't come any more, and the next day the twenty-third fairy said there was a queer-shaped leaf on the watercress down by the spring, and he thought he ought to look round a bit and see if there were any more like it, and he couldn't come any more.

And so it went on until Gillibloom was the only one left, and he sat by the Standing Pool and dished up water to splash his face and wrinkled up his forehead and shut his eyes and drew down his mouth and bellowed; and whenever the rest of the fairies heard him or saw him, they clapped their hands over their eyes, and put their fingers in their ears, and ran away as hard as they could. And so it happened that the forest about the Standing Pool was perfectly quiet, for no bird or squirrel or bee or any other thing that lives and breathes in the forest will stay after the fairies are gone.

And the Sun looked in and said: "There is nobody there but that silly Gillibloom, and he is Almost Crying all the time. I'll go away somewhere else."

And the Moon looked down at night and said: "Why, there's nothing in that forest but a Dreadful Sound. There's no use in my troubling myself to squeeze down through the branches, for sounds can get along just as well by themselves."

So she drove off very fast to the fairy green, and rolled such a river of light into the fairy ring that the fairies gave up dancing, and got flower-cups and sailed on the river, and some who couldn't stop to get flower-cups swam in it, and it was the gayest night ever to be remembered.

Now, when Gillibloom found that the fairies had all gone and left him to himself, and the four-footed things and the two-footed things, and the things that have feathers and fur and gauze-wings and shell-wings had gone too, he had felt differently from what he ever had before. He had been bellowing for a long time that night, because he was determined to learn to cry and get it over, and then go back to his people, but now he said to himself: "I will not cry any more. And anyway it is not Quite Crying, and if Almost Crying makes everything run away from me, I don't know what Quite Crying would do."

So he tried to shut his mouth, and stop its bellowing, but it would not stop. And he tried to smooth his forehead, and it stayed wrinkled, and he tried to draw up the corners of his mouth, and they would not stay, and he tried to open his eyes, and they would not open. And there was a strange feeling in his throat, and his heart beat very fast, and though he had not dipped up the water of the Standing Pool for as much as two hours, his cheeks were all wet.

"Oh," said Gillibloom to himself, "what has happened to me! what has happened to me!"

And he started running as fast as he could through the silent forest to the Earth-Woman's house, and as he ran he said to himself: "What has happened to me? What has happened to me? Am I afraid?"

Now for a fairy to be afraid is just as impossible as for it not to be a fairy, but Gillibloom knew he was somehow changed, and he could only run and call aloud at the top of his voice, "Am I afraid? Am I afraid?"

Now the Earth-Woman lives in the very middle of the wood, in a green house that nobody can see by day, and a dark brown house that nobody can see by night. And when she heard Gillibloom come screaming through the forest, she stepped to her door and stood waiting for him, and in a minute he was there, and laid hold of her skirts and clung to them.

"Well! Well!" said the Earth-Woman, "and who is this?" Then she stooped down and took up Gillibloom between her thumb and forefinger, and looked at him. "By acorns and nuts!" said she. "It's the Cry Fairy."

"No! no!" said Gillibloom. "No! no! I'm the Almost Cry Fairy. I'm never going to Quite Cry, for I don't know what it would do to me."

The Earth-Woman laid her finger to Gillibloom's cheek and touched it and put it, all wet, to her lips. She nodded and then shook her head.

"Well," said she, "you were a silly, weren't you? Now what do you want me to do?"

Gillibloom kept on bellowing.

"I want to be with the others."

"What others?" asked the Earth-Woman severely. "The other cry-babies?"

"The fairies and the furs and the feathers and the wings and the fins and the tails and the sun and the moon," bellowed Gillibloom, though now you could hardly have understood a word he said.

But the Earth-Woman could understand. She understood everything.

"Then," she said, "you must open your eyes, smooth out your forehead and pull up your mouth, and stop that noise."

Gillibloom tried, because, whatever the Earth-Woman says in the forest, it has to be done. But he could not do it. And worse than that, he found he didn't really want to.

"Do you like to have your throat feel all pinched up, as if you couldn't swallow a drop of honey?" the Earth-Woman asked him.

"No!" screamed Gillibloom. And then he roared louder than ever. You could have heard him across twenty violets.

"Do you like to have your mouth all salt with tears, and your pretty tunic wet with them?"

"No! No!" said Gillibloom.

But he kept on roaring.

"There, you see!" said the Earth-Woman. "Now I'll tell you something, Gillibloom, and you keep it in your mind until you forget it. The more you cry, the harder it is to stop, and the only way to stop crying is to smile."

"Cry?" said Gillibloom. "Is this Quite Crying? Isn't it Almost Crying?"

"That's as may be," said the Earth-Woman wisely. "Now you come in here with me."

So she carried him into her hut, where it is very dark but light enough to see to do all sorts of wonderful things, and she ironed out his forehead and put a nice polish on it, and she opened his eyes and told them to stay open, and she shut his mouth and told it to stay shut, and when it had really done it, she stretched it very carefully indeed, until it was perhaps two cat's hairs wider than it had been for a long time.

"There!" said she, "I can't do any more until it softens a little. Lie down there, Gillibloom, and think about leaves in spring."

So Gillibloom lay down on a very soft couch that was perhaps rose-leaves and perhaps thistledown and perhaps cornsilk, and when he had lain there a day and a night, the Earth-Woman stretched his mouth a little more, and a little more. And one night she said to him: "Now, Gillibloom, your cure will take quite a long time yet, but you must do the rest of it yourself. And this is what you must do. Whenever you think of crying, you must stretch your mouth just as wide as you can."

"Why, that's what the mortals call smiling," said Gillibloom.

"And you must keep on doing it until you've forgotten to cry. Now. I wish you were in the fairy ring."

And she had no sooner said it than he was there. All the fairies were dancing the new dance that is called, "Remember the Robins and Roses To-day and Think of the Lilies and Larks." Now when they saw Gillibloom standing there among them, balancing on one foot and trying to look very bold and gay, they stopped dancing and half turned away, and looked at him over their shoulders. If Gillibloom was going to teach, they didn't propose to stay more than a second and a half in his company.

Gillibloom looked very nice. The Earth-Woman had got the salt stains out of his tunic, and pressed it neatly for him, and brought him a new pair of grasshopper tights. They were very much worn at that time. And he was stretching his mouth as hard as he could, and he put up one hand and touched his cheek, and it was quite dry. That gave him courage.

"Come on, fellows," he said. "On with the dance!"

Just then the moon looked down, and she was so pleased to see Gillibloom back again that she tossed a moon-wreath down over his shoulders, and it brightened up the old tunic wonderfully and sent a splendid light up into his face. And the fairies could see he was smiling, and they began singing together.

"Gillibloom!" they sang, "Gillibloom! Gillibloom's come back!"

DOLL-IN-THE-GRASS

Once upon a time there was a king who had twelve sons. When they were grown big, he told them they must go out into the world and win themselves wives, but these wives must be able to spin, and weave, and sew a shirt in one day. If they could not, he would not have them for daughters-in-law.

To each son he gave a horse and a new suit of clothes, and they went out into the world to look for brides. When they had gone a little way together, they said that they would not have Boots, their youngest brother, with them, for he was stupid.

So Boots had to stay behind, and he did not know what to do or where to turn. He became very downcast, and got off his horse, and sat down in the tall grass to think. But after he had sat there a while, one of the tufts in the grass began to stir and move, and out of it came a little white thing. When it came nearer, Boots saw that it was a charming little lassie, and such a tiny bit of a thing, no larger than a small doll.

The lassie went up to Boots and asked him if he would like to come down and call on her, and she said that her name was Doll-in-the-Grass.

Boots said that he would be greatly pleased to accept her invitation. When he leaned down a little closer, there sat Doll-in-the-Grass on a chair. She was the tiniest lassie you can imagine, and very, very beautiful. She asked Boots where he was going, and what was his business. So he told her how there were twelve brothers of them, and how the king had told each one of them to go out into the world and find himself a wife who could spin, and weave, and sew a shirt all in one day.

"But if you will only say at once that you will be my wife," Boots said to Doll-in-the-Grass, "I will not go a step farther."

She was willing, and so she made haste and spun, and wove, and sewed the shirt, but it was very, very tiny. It was no more than two inches long. Boots went off home with it, but when he took it out he was almost ashamed of it, it was so small. But the king was pleased with it, and said he should have her. So Boots set off, glad and happy, to fetch the little lassie.

When he came to Doll-in-the-Grass, he wished to take her up before him on his horse. But she would not have that, for she said she would sit and drive along in a silver spoon, and that she had two white horses to draw it. So off they started, Boots on his horse, and Doll-in-the-Grass in her silver spoon;

and the two horses that drew her were two tiny white mice. But Boots always kept on the other side of the road, for he was afraid lest he should ride over her, she was so little.

When they had gone a little way they came to a great piece of water. Here Boots' horse grew frightened, and shied across the road. The spoon upset, and Doll-in-the-Grass tumbled into the water. Then Boots was in great distress, for he did not know how to get her out again; but, suddenly, up came a merman with her. How wonderful; Doll-in-the-Grass was now as tall and well grown as other girls! So Boots took her up before him on his horse, and rode home.

All Boots' brothers had come back with their sweethearts, but not one had woven so dainty a little shirt as had Doll-in-the-Grass, and none was half so lovely. When the brothers saw her they were as jealous as could be of their brother. But the king was so delighted with her that he gave them the finest wedding feast of all. He allowed them to live with him in his palace, and gave out word that they should succeed him on the throne.

FABLES

THE PLOUGHMAN AND HIS SONS

A wealthy Ploughman, drawing near his end,Called in his sons apart from every friend,And said, "When of your sire bereft,The heritage your father leftGuard well, nor sell a single field.A treasure in it is concealed.The place, precisely, I don't know,But industry will serve to show.The harvest past, Time's forelock take,And search with plough, and spade, and rake;Turn over every inch of sod,Nor leave unsearched a single clod!"The father died. The sons in vainTurned o'er the soil, and o'er again.That year their acres boreMore grain than e'er before.Though hidden money found they none,Yet had their father wisely done,To show by such a measureThat toil itself is treasure.

The farmer's patient care and toilAre oftener wanting than the soil.

THE BAG OF DUST

There was once a prince who went to his father, the King, to receive his fortune. And when the King ordered it to be brought in, what do you think it was—a great, gray bag of dust!

The Prince, now that he was old enough to go out in the world, had expected a very different fortune from this—a Kingdom all his own in some other land, a chest of jewels, and a gold crown.

But his father, the King, helped the Prince to put the bag of dust, which was very heavy indeed, upon his back.

"You are to carry this to the boundary line of the Kingdom without once dropping it," he said. And the Prince, who always did what his father, the King, said, set out.

It seemed as if the bag grew heavier at every step. The Prince had not known that dust could weigh so much. It sifted out of the coarse bag and covered his fine velvet cloak so that you could not have told him from the poorest subject in the Kingdom. The folk in the streets laughed at him, and the dogs barked at his heels.

Before the Prince had gone very far he came to a field where all the princes from the Kingdoms near by were playing games and riding their beautiful horses. The Prince stopped a moment, because he wanted to join them. He could ride a horse without a saddle, and hit the centre of a target with his bow and arrow. But as he stopped he remembered the bag of dust upon his back which his father, the King, had said that he must not set down.

So he started on again, but the bag was heavier now.

He had not gone much farther, when he came to a beautiful park, set in the midst of a green forest. There were rustic seats, placed beneath trees whose branches hung low with ripe fruit of all kinds. Some one must have known that the Prince was coming, for a table was set for him with sweets and other fruits and all manner of dainty things to eat. The Prince was very hungry, for it was long past noon and he had eaten nothing. He was about to sit down at the table when he remembered the bag of dust upon his back. He knew that he must not set it down.

So he started on again, but the bag was even heavier now.

He went on, farther and farther, and the way was strange to him now, for he had come a long way. The bag seemed to grow larger with every step that he took; it covered his back, and bent his shoulders, and bowed his head. Although he had come so far, he seemed no nearer the boundary of the Kingdom than he had been when he started out. Suddenly he saw, like a white cloud in front of him, a great lovely castle.

There was no one in the pretty rose garden in front save soft-eyed deer. There was no one looking out of the bright windows, or at the door which stood wide open. It seemed as if the castle was waiting for the Prince and, because he was very tired from carrying his load of dust so far, he went through the garden and up to the door. But, just as he was going inside, he discovered that the door was not large enough to let his bag through, too, and he knew that he must not set it down.

So he started on again, but the bag was heavier than it had ever been before.

On and on went the Prince, but he felt like an old man and his steps were slow because he was so tired. He wanted to turn back, and he wanted to set down his load, but his father, the King, had said that he must carry it to the boundary of the Kingdom. The day was almost done, but it seemed as if he would never reach it.

Suddenly, though, he came to the end of the road and looked over the edge of the Kingdom.

There was a castle, not white, but gold. All about it were more beautiful gardens than those which he had left behind. In the door stood his father, the King, come in his chariot by another road to welcome him.

"Set down your bag," said the King, so the Prince did and he felt suddenly rested and young again.

"Look inside it," said the King. So the Prince looked inside the bag, and he found out what had made it so heavy.

Each grain of dust had turned to gold!

THE CAMEL AND THE PIG

A Camel and a Pig chanced to meet in a far country, and as neither had seen the other before, they began at once to boast.

"The greatest distinction and the most good in the world comes from being tall," said the Camel. "Look at me, Pig; behold how tall I am!"

The Pig looked at the Camel, so far above him in height, but he had made up his mind not to be outdone by him.

"You are in the wrong, Camel," argued the Pig. "There is nothing in the world so important as being short. Look at me, and behold how short I am!"

The Camel looked down at the Pig but he was not of his opinion. "This matter must be settled by a test," he said. "If I fail to prove the truth of what I feel about myself, I will give up my hump."

"That is well spoken," replied the Pig. "And if I cannot show you the truth of what I have said I will give up my snout."

"It is a bargain!" said the Camel.

"Agreed!" said the Pig.

So the Camel and the Pig started on a journey together to find out which of the two was the more honorable, and in the course of time they came to a garden. It was entirely surrounded by a low stone wall in which there was no opening.

The Camel stood beside the wall and looked at the green plants, growing in such profusion inside the garden. Then he stretched his long neck over the wall and ate a hearty breakfast of juicy green leaves and stalks. Then he turned and jeered at the Pig who stood at the bottom of the wall and could not catch a glimpse even of the good things in the garden.

"Which would you rather be, Pig, tall or short?" asked the Camel as they travelled on again, and the Pig did not answer.

Soon, though, they came to a second garden, enclosed by a very high wall. At one end there was a wicket gate. The Pig quickly squeezed himself under the gate and went into the garden. He ate a hearty meal of the ripe vegetables that he found there, and came out, laughing in his turn at the Camel who had not been able to reach over the wall.

"Which would you rather be, Camel, short, or tall?" asked the Pig, and the Camel did not answer.

So the two thought the matter over and they decided that the Camel had reason to keep his hump and the Pig to keep his snout. For it is good to be tall when height is needed; and it is also important, at times, to be short.

LEGENDS

HOW THE MOON WAS KIND TO HER MOTHER

Once upon a time, a long, long while ago, the Sun, the Wind, and the Moon were three sisters, and their mother was a pale, lovely Star that shone, far away, in the dark evening sky.

One day their uncle and aunt, who were no more or less than the Thunder and Lightning, asked the three sisters to have supper with them, and their mother said that they might go. She would wait for them, she said, and would not set until all three returned and told her about their pleasant visit.

So the Sun in her dress of gold, the Wind in a trailing dress that rustled as she passed, and the Moon in a wonderful gown of silver started out for the party with the Thunder and Lightning. Oh, it was a supper to remember! The table was spread with a cloth of rainbow. There were ices like the snow on the mountain tops, and cakes as soft and white as clouds, and fruits from every quarter of the earth. The three sisters ate their fill, especially the Sun and the Wind, who were very greedy, and left not so much as a crumb on their plates. But the Moon was kind and remembered her mother. She hid a part of her supper in her long, white fingers to take home and share with her mother, the Star.

Then the three sisters said good-bye to the Thunder and Lightning and went home. When they reached there, they found their mother, the Star, waiting and shining for them as she had said she would.

"What did you bring me from the supper?" she asked.

The Sun tossed her head with all its yellow hair in disdain as she answered her mother.

"Why should I bring you anything?" she asked. "I went out for my own pleasure and not to think of you."

It was the same with the Wind. She wrapped her flowing robes about her and turned away from her mother.

"I, too, went out for my own entertainment," she said, "and why should I think of you, mother, when you were not with me?"

But it was very different with the Moon who was not greedy and selfish as her two sisters, the Sun and the Wind, were. She turned her pale sweet face toward her mother, the Star, and held out her slender hands.

"See, mother," cried the Moon, "I have brought you part of everything that was on my plate. I ate only half of the feast for I wanted to share it with you."

So the mother brought a gold plate and the food that her unselfish daughter, the Moon, had brought her heaped the plate high. She ate it, and then she turned to her three children, for she had something important to say to them. She spoke first to the Sun.

"You were thoughtless and selfish, my daughter," she said. "You went out and enjoyed yourself with no thought of one who was left alone at home. Hereafter you shall be no longer beloved among men. Your rays shall be so hot and burning that they shall scorch everything they touch. Men shall cover their heads when you appear, and they shall run away from you."

And that is why, to this day, the Sun is hot and blazing.

Next the mother spoke to the Wind.

"You, too, my daughter, have been unkind and greedy," she said. "You, also, enjoyed yourself with no thought of any one else. You shall blow in the parching heat of your sister, the Sun, and wither and blast all that you touch. No one shall love you any longer, but all men will dislike and avoid you."

And that is why, to this day, the Wind, blowing in hot weather, is so unpleasant.

But, last, the mother spoke to her kind daughter, the Moon.

"You remembered your mother, and were unselfish," she said. "To those who are thoughtful of their mother, great blessings come. For all time your light shall be cool, and calm, and beautiful. You shall wane, but you shall wax again. You shall make the dark night bright, and all men shall call you blessed."

And that is why, to this day, the Moon is so cool, and bright, and beautiful.

THE RABBIT WHO WAS GRATEFUL

Everything in the woods was covered deep with snow, the berries, the juicy young bushes, and the roots. The animals had stowed themselves away for the winter to sleep; the bear in a deep cave, the chipmunk in a hollow log, and the wild mouse in a cozy hole beneath the roots of a tree. The wind sang a high, shrill song in the tops of the pine trees, and the doors of the wigwams were shut tight.

But the door of Son-of-a-Brave's wigwam suddenly opened a little way and the Indian boy, himself, looked out. He had his bow and a newly tipped arrow in his hands.

While the snow and the ice had been piling up outside in the Indian village, Son-of-a-Brave had been very busy working beside the home fire making his new arrow head. First, he had gone to the wigwam of the village arrow maker to ask him for a piece of stone, and the arrow maker had been good enough to give Son-of-a-Brave a piece of beautiful white quartz. Then Son-of-a-Brave had set to work on it. He had shaped it with a big horn knife and chipped it with a hammer. He had polished it in a dish of sand until it shone like one of the icicles outside. Then he had fitted it to a strong arrow and wished that he had a chance to shoot. That was why Son-of-a-Brave stood at the entrance of the wigwam, looking out across the snow that not even a deer had tracked because the winter was so severe.

All at once Son-of-a-Brave saw something. An old hare struggled out of a snow bank and limped down the path that led by the wigwam. In the summer the hare was gray, the color of the trees among which he lived, but in the winter he turned white so as not to be seen by hunters when he went along through the snow. He did not think now, however, whether any one saw him or not. He was a very old hare indeed, and the winter was proving too hard for him. He was lame and hungry and half frozen. He stopped right in front of Son-of-a-Brave and sat up on his haunches, his ears drooping.

"Don't shoot me," he was trying to say. "I am at your mercy, too starved to run away from you."

Son-of-a-Brave slipped his newly tipped arrow in his bow and aimed at the old hare. It would be very easy indeed to shoot him, for the hare did not move, and the boy thought what a warm pair of moccasin tops his skin would make. Then Son-of-a-Brave took his arrow out again, for another thought had come to him. He knew that it would be cowardly to shoot a hare that was too weak to run away.

The boy stooped down and picked up the old hare, wrapping him up close to his own warm body in his blanket. Then he went with him through the snow of the woods until they came to a place where a stream lay, and there were young willow trees growing along the edge. Here he set down the hare, and began to dig away the ice and frozen earth with his new arrow tip until the roots of the trees could be seen, and the soft bark. How the hare did eat these! As Son-of-a-Brave left him and went home, he could still see the famished creature nibbling the food for which he had been so hungry.

The Indian boy never saw the hare again that winter. He knew that he had dug a large enough hole so that the hare could find shelter and have enough food. His bow and arrow were hung on the wall, and Son-of-a-Brave sat by the fire with his mother and father until spring came.

One day a bird sang out in the forest. Then the streams began to sing, and the moss that made a carpet all over the ground outside the wigwam was again green. Son-of-a-Brave felt like running and shouting. He left off his blanket and went out into the woods to play.

He had scarcely gone a rod from the wigwam when he saw a large gray hare, following him. This was strange for one usually ran away. Son-of-a-Brave waited, and the hare came close to him. Then he saw, because it limped, that it was the old hare that he had befriended in the winter, but fat and well fed, and dressed in his summer coat.

The hare flopped his ears to Son-of-a-Brave and hopped a little way ahead, so the boy followed. He went on, without stopping, until he came to the very spot beside the stream where Son-of-a-Brave had dug away the snow with his new arrow head to give the hare food.

Oh, what did the boy see there!

Blossoming out of the bare earth were beautiful flowers, as white outside as a hare's ears in the winter time, and pink inside, like their lining. They had a sweet perfume, different from anything that had grown in the woods before. The grateful hare stood beside them and seemed to be trying to say that these new flowers were his gift to the boy who had helped him.

The Indian story tellers say that those were the first Mayflowers, and that they have been blossoming in the woods ever since because the hare brought them out of thankfulness to Son-of-a-Brave.

WHY THE BEES GATHER HONEY

Once upon a time, when it was the story age, and things were very different from what they are now, two tribes of pygmies lived very near each other.

These tribes of little people looked just alike, they both were very, very tiny, and they both lived out of doors in the fields. But in one respect they were quite different. One tribe of little folks spent a great deal of time gathering food of all kinds from the woods and the wild orchards, and storing it away for the winter. The other tribe of little people never harvested or saved at all; they spent all their time playing.

"Come and have a good time with us; winter is a long way off, and you are wasting these sunny days," the lazy pygmies would call to the industrious ones. But the busy pygmies always made the same reply to their little neighbors,

"It is you who are wasting these days. Winter may be far away, but it will be cold and barren when it does come. Everything will be covered deep with snow, and what will we eat if we do not harvest now?"

But the lazy little people danced, and sang, and played on all summer. "Why should we think of the winter?" they said to one another. "Our neighbors who are gathering food so busily will probably have a large enough store for two tribes. They will feed us."

And that is just what happened. When the snow flew, and the lazy pygmies were almost at the point of starving, their kind little neighbors brought them pots of wild honey on which they feasted and grew fat.

Then another summer came. Like all industrious folk, the working pygmies planned to accomplish more that season than they had the year before.

"If we move, so as to live nearer the wild flowers, we can gather more honey," they said. And the whole tribe of industrious little people went to another field where wild roses and lilies, dripping with nectar, grew.

At first the lazy pygmies did not even miss their kind little neighbors. They danced, and sang, and played again through all the long, bright summer days. When it grew cold, and they had to hide themselves to escape the frost and had no food, they said,

"What does it matter? Our friends will come back to us soon with supplies for the winter."

It was too long a journey, though, for the little workers to take through the snow. The days grew more and more cold, and storms swept the earth. The lazy little people cried out in their hunger to the manito, the spirit who watched all outdoors, to come and help them.

So the manito came, but first he went to the industrious tribe of little folk to reward them.

"You shall have wings," the manito said, "to take you from flower to flower that you may gather honey with ease. You shall be called honey bees, and, as you fly, you shall hum so that mortals may hear you and take pattern from your industry. All your life long, you shall live on honey."

Then the manito visited the lazy pygmies. "You, too, shall have wings," he said, "but they shall be to carry you away as mortals drive you from place to place. You shall have buzzing voices to tell mortals you are near that they may kill you. Your food shall be only that which is thrown away. You are the despised flies."

And ever since then the bees have gathered honey, and the flies have been killed in memory of the day when one tribe of little people was busy and kind, and the other tribe indolent and selfish.

BIRTHDAYS

THE BIRTHDAY PRESENT

One afternoon, as Mother sat out on the long porch paring apples, the children came running in. There were Cousin Pen, who was visiting at the farm, and Brother Fred, and little Ben, and they all began to talk at the same time.

"To-morrow is Grandmother's birthday," they cried. "What can we give her for a birthday present?"

"I think a silk dress would be nice if we had enough money to buy it," said Cousin Pen.

"Let's give her a watermelon, the biggest one we can find," said Brother Fred.

"Or one of the new kittens; Grandmother likes cats," said little Ben.

"A roll of fresh butter, as yellow as gold and as sweet as clover," said Mother, "if you will do the churning yourselves."

"Oh, yes, we will churn," promised the children, and they ran off to their play, well satisfied, for they could think of nothing nicer than a roll of fresh butter, as yellow as gold and as sweet as clover, for Grandmother's birthday present.

By and by the cows came home. Their names were Daisy and Dandelion and Dolly, and as soon as the children heard the tinkle of their bells in the lane they made haste to open the big back gate, for it was milking time.

Father milked, and when he carried his buckets of sweet white milk to the house, Mother strained the milk into the bright tin pans that stood in a row on the dairy room shelves. The next afternoon every pan was covered with thick yellow cream, all ready for the churning. Mother skimmed the cream into the great stone churn.

"Who will churn first?" she asked.

"I will," said Cousin Pen. "I like to make the dasher go dancing up and down."

So Cousin Pen put on one of Mother's gingham aprons and began to churn. "It is easy to churn," she said at first, but after a little her arms grew tired and the dasher grew heavy. She did not think of giving up, though, for she was churning to get her Grandmother's birthday butter, and the dasher seemed to say to her as it splashed up and down:

Oh, the cream to butter's turning,In the churning, churning, churning.It will turn, turn, turn,As you churn, churn, churn,All the cream to butter turning,In the churning, churning, churning.

"Brother Fred's turn," called Mother, and Brother Fred came running up the kitchen steps to take the dasher from Cousin Pen.

"I think it is fun to churn. I don't believe I will ever get tired," he said.

He did get tired, but he would not stop even to rest, for he was churning to get his Grandmother's birthday butter, and the dasher seemed to say to him:

Hear the buttermilk a-bumming,For the yellow butter's coming.It will come, come, come,With a bum, bum, bum,All the buttermilk a-bumming,When the yellow butter's coming.

"Little Ben's turn," called Mother. Little Ben had to stand on a box to churn, and his cheeks were as red as roses as he worked away.

"Don't you want us to help you?" asked the other children.

"No, indeed," said little Ben; "I guess I can churn to get my Grandmother some birthday butter," and he churned with a will, till the dasher seemed to say to him:

Bum, bum,Butter's come.

Mother looked in the churn and, sure enough, the flakes of golden butter were floating on the milk.

"Hurrah!" cried little Ben. "Hurrah!" cried Cousin Pen and Brother Fred, and they hurried into the kitchen to watch Mother as she gathered the butter, and worked it, and salted it, and patted it into a very fine roll. When she had done that she printed a star on top of the roll, and the butter was ready to take to Grandmother.

"You must make Grandmother guess what it is," said Mother as she put the butter into a nice little basket and covered it with a white napkin.

"All right," said the children; so when they got to Grandmother's house they called, "Grandmother, Grandmother, guess what we have brought you for a birthday present."

"It is yellow as gold," said Brother Fred.

"It's sweet as clover," said Cousin Pen.

"We churned it ourselves," said little Ben; and Grandmother guessed what it was with her very first guess.

"It is just what I wanted," she said, and she kissed them every one. She had been thinking about them, too, all the long day, and she had baked a beautiful cake for their tea.

Mother and Father came to tea, and all together they had the best birthday party they had ever known.

The children thought the birthday cake was the nicest that they had ever tasted, but Grandmother said she thought nothing could be nicer than her birthday butter.

THE BIRTHDAY OF THE INFANTA

It was the birthday of the Infanta. She was just twelve years old, and the sun shone brightly in the garden of the palace.

On ordinary days, she was only allowed to play with children of her own rank, but on this, her birthday, the King had given orders that she was to invite any one whom she liked to amuse her. So she had many children with whom to play, but she was the most beautiful of them all. Her robe was of gray satin, embroidered with silver and studded with pearls. Two tiny slippers with big pink rosettes peeped out beneath her dress as she walked. Pink and pearl was her great gauze fan, and in her hair, which, like an aureole of gold, stood out stiffly around her pale little face, she had a beautiful white rose.

The Infanta watched her companions play hide and seek round the stone vases and the old moss-grown statues of the garden. Then a procession of noble boys came out to meet her and led her solemnly to a little gilt and ivory chair that was placed on a raised dais above an arena. The children grouped themselves all round, laughing and whispering, for the Infanta's birthday sports were now to begin.

There was a marvellous bull fight in which some of the boys pranced about on richly caparisoned hobby horses and vanquished a bull made of wicker work and stretched hide. Next came the puppet show, and then a juggler who played on a curious reed pipe for two green and gold snakes to dance. He made a tiny orange tree grow out of sand, and blossom and bear fruit; and he took the Infanta's fan and changed it into a bluebird that flew about and sang. Then a shaggy brown bear and some little apes were brought in. The bear stood on his head, and the apes fought with tiny swords and went through a regular soldiers' drill like the King's own bodyguard.

But the funniest part of the whole morning's entertainment was undoubtedly the dancing of the little dwarf.

When he stumbled into the arena, waddling on his crooked legs and wagging his huge misshapen head from side to side, the children went off into a loud shout of delight; and the Infanta, herself, laughed so much that one of the Court ladies had to remind her that such merriment was not befitting a princess.

It was the dwarf's first appearance, too. He had been discovered only the day before, running wild in the forest, and had been brought to the palace to surprise the Infanta. His father, a poor charcoal burner, was pleased to get rid of so ugly and useless a child. Perhaps the most amusing thing about the little dwarf was his happiness. He did not know how ugly he was; he did not know that he was a dwarf.

When the children laughed, he laughed as joyously as any of them. At the close of each dance he made the funniest bows, smiling and nodding to them just as if he were one of them. As for the Infanta, he could not keep his eyes off her and seemed to dance for her alone. When, in jest, she took the beautiful white rose out of her hair and threw it at him, the dwarf put his hand on his heart and knelt before her, his little bright eyes sparkling with pleasure.

The Infanta laughed at him until long after he had run out of the arena, and she commanded that his dance be immediately repeated. But it was growing warm in the garden. The Infanta was reminded that a wonderful feast awaited her, including a birthday cake with her initials worked all over it in painted sugar, and a lovely silver flag waving in the top. So she rose with great dignity, and gave orders that the little dwarf should perform before her again, after she had taken her nap.

Now when the little dwarf heard that he was to dance a second time before the Infanta, he was so proud that he ran about the garden, kissing the white rose in his great delight. She had given him her beautiful rose; she must love him, he thought. Perhaps she would put him at her right hand in the throne room and let him be her playmate, for, although the dwarf had never been in a palace before, he knew a great many wonderful things.

He could make little cages out of rushes for the grasshoppers to sing in, and he knew where the wood pigeon built her nest. All the wild dances he knew: the swift dance in a red mantle with the autumn, the light dance in blue sandals over the corn, the dance with white snow wreaths in the winter, and the blossom dance through the orchards in the spring. The Infanta would love his forest friends, too, the rabbits that scurried about in the fern, the hedgehogs that could curl themselves up into prickly balls, and the great wise tortoises that crawled slowly about, nibbling the leaves and shaking their heads. Yes, she must certainly come to the forest to play with him!

He would give her his own little bed, and would watch outside the window until dawn to see that the wolves did not creep too near the hut. Then, in the morning, he would tap at the shutters and wake her, and they would go out and play together all day long.

But where was the Infanta?

The whole palace seemed asleep. The dwarf wandered around looking for some place through which he might gain an entrance, and at last he caught sight of a small door that was lying open. He slipped through, and found himself in a splendid hall. He followed it to the end, slipping through velvet curtains from one gilded room to another, each one more magnificent than the last. Here was another room, the brightest and most beautiful of all. The walls were patterned with birds and dotted with silver blossoms. The furniture was of heavy silver festooned with wreaths. It seemed as if the Infanta must run across the pale green floor to meet him. At last he discovered that he was no longer alone in the palace. Standing under the shadow of the doorway, at the extreme end of the room, he saw a little figure watching him. His heart trembled, a cry of joy broke from his lips, and he moved out into the sunlight. As he did so, the figure moved out also, and the little dwarf saw it plainly.

The Infanta? No, it was a monster; not properly shaped as all other people were, but with a crooked back and limbs! The little dwarf frowned and the monster frowned. He struck at it, and it returned blow for blow. What was it, he asked himself? He took the Infanta's rose from his coat and kissed it to comfort himself, for he was afraid. The monster had a rose, too, and kissed it also.

So the truth came to the little dwarf. It was he who was misshapen and ugly to look at; a mirror had shown him. He could not bear it and he fell, crying, to the floor.

At that moment the Infanta, herself, came in through the open door, and when she saw the ugly little dwarf lying on the ground and beating it with his clenched hands, she went off into shouts of happy laughter.

"His dancing was funny," said the Infanta, "but his acting is funnier still. He is almost as good as the puppets," and she clapped her hands.

But the little dwarf never looked up, and his sobs grew fainter and fainter, and suddenly he gave a curious gasp and clutched his side. And then he fell back, and lay quite still.

"That was splendid!" said the Infanta, "and now you must get up and dance for me!"

But the little dwarf made no answer.

The Infanta stamped her foot, and called to the Court Chamberlain.

"My funny little dwarf is sulking," she cried. "You must wake him up and tell him to dance for me!"

So the Chamberlain came in from the terrace where he had been walking and bent over the dwarf, tapping him on his cheek with his embroidered glove.

But the little dwarf never moved.

The Chamberlain looked grave, and he knelt beside the dwarf, putting his hand on his heart. And after a few moments he rose up, and making a low bow to the Infanta, said,

"My beautiful Princess, your funny little dwarf will never dance again. It is a pity, for he is so ugly that he might have made the King smile."

"But why will he not dance again?" asked the Infanta, laughing.

"Because his heart is broken," answered the Chamberlain.

And the Infanta frowned, and her rose-leaf lips curled in scorn. "For the future let those who come to play with me have no hearts," she cried, and she ran out into the garden.

THE PRICKLY BUSH

It was the only growing thing in the whole, beautiful garden that was prickly. It stood beside the sunny path, so low that the white rabbit could jump over it. It longed to spread its branches across the path to be touched by the gardener and the children, but no one cared to go very near the little bush that was so covered with thorns.

The day lily had broad, soft leaves without a single thorn. It spread them away from the prickly bush. The tulips had tall, smooth leaves. They held them very high, and away from the bush that was so full of thorns. The white rabbit that lived in the garden and loved to sun himself beneath the plants was very careful not to go near the prickly little bush.

"I must tie this bush so that it cannot hurt any one," the gardener said one day as he passed it. "The thorns on it are growing larger and larger every day." So he cut a long, straight stick, and painted it green, and stuck it in the ground beside the prickly little bush. Then he tied the bush tightly to the stick, which kept it from leaning over the path.

"Be very careful not to go near that ugly little bush," said the children to each other. "It will scratch you even worse than the cat scratches."

All this was very discouraging, and the prickly little bush drooped and did not feel like growing.

The days of the summer grew warmer, the sun shone, and soft rains fell upon the garden. A pleasant breeze came singing down the path, and the sun, and the rain, and the breeze, each one, spoke to the prickly little bush.

"Climb up a little higher," the great, yellow sun seemed to say. So the prickly little bush pulled and stretched its prickly branches up toward the blue sky, and as it grew higher and higher, its thorns went, too, out of the way of the rabbit and the children.

"Push harder," the pattering raindrops seemed to say to the roots of the prickly little bush as they soaked down through the ground. So the roots of the prickly little bush pushed, and pushed until the branches seemed bursting, and green leaves and tiny buds came and covered over the thorns so that they could scarcely be seen at all.

"Open your buds as wide as you can," the warm breezes seemed to sing as they stopped in the branches of the prickly little bush. So the little bush unfolded its brown buds as wide and as prettily as it could.

Then it came to be the most beautiful day of all, the mother's birthday. The children went out to the garden to try to find the loveliest thing that grew there to be their mother's birthday gift. And that was not easy because the garden was so full of lovely things.

"I am sure that she will like this tall white lily," said one of the children.

"But the lily fades so quickly after it is picked," said another child. "I think that she would like a red tulip."

"But our mother loves pink better than she loves red," said the youngest child. "Do let us go on a little farther before we decide what to take her for her birthday. Oh, how pretty — " The youngest child stopped in front of the prickly little bush, and the others crowded close to see, too.

They never would have known that it was the prickly bush, at all. It stood as proudly and as straight as a little tree, and its green leaves covered it like a beautiful dress. Peeping out from between the leaves were the most lovely pink flowers, as soft as velvet and with so many curling petals that one could not count them. They smelled more sweetly than any other flower in the garden, and the children could scarcely speak at first, they were so surprised.

"Roses!" said one child.

"Pink roses!" said another child.

"The prickly little bush has turned into a rose bush for our mother's birthday," said the youngest child.

So they smelled of the beautiful pink roses, and touched them to feel how soft and like velvet the petals were. Then they decided that the pink roses that had bloomed on the prickly little bush were the loveliest flowers in the whole garden, and they picked the largest pink rose of all to carry into the house for their mother's birthday gift.

On the way they met the gardener, and they showed him the beautiful rose, telling him how it had grown upon the prickly little bush. He smiled, for he knew a great deal about the strange ways of his plants.

"I thought it would bear roses this year," the gardener said. "It often happens that the bush with the sharpest thorns to carry, once it blooms, has the prettiest roses."

ARBOR DAY

THE TINKER'S WILLOW

One day, when my Grandfather Gifford was about seven years old, he looked across the road to his father's blacksmith shop, and seeing some one sitting on the bench by the door, went over to learn who it was.

He found a little old man, with thick, bushy eyebrows and bright blue eyes. His clothes were made all of leather, which creaked and rattled when he moved. By his side was a partly open pack, in which grandfather could see curious tools and sheets of shiny tin. By that he knew that the man was the travelling tinker, who came once or twice a year to mend leaky pans and pails, and of whom he had heard his mother speak.

The old man was eating his luncheon—a slice or two of bread, a bit of cold meat, and a cold potato; and because it seemed so poor a luncheon, grandfather went back to the house and brought two big apples from the cellar. The old man thanked him and ate the apples. Then he got up, brushed the bread crumbs from his leather breeches, and taking a little tin dipper from his pack, went down to the brook for a drink of water. When he had had his fill, he came back to the bench and sat down.

"Now, my boy," he said, "we will make a tree to grow here by the brook. There ought to be one, for shade."

"Make a tree!" cried grandfather. "How can we make a tree? I thought only God made trees."

"True," said the old man. "Only God makes trees, but sometimes we can help Him."

With that, he took from the bench at his side a stick that he had cut somewhere by the road, and had been using for a cane. It was slender and straight, and grandfather noticed that the bark was smooth and of a beautiful light green.

"Of this," said the old man, "we will make a tree in which the birds of the air shall build their nests, and under which the beasts of the field shall find shelter, and rest in the heat of the day. But first there shall be music, to please the spirits of the springtime. Take this stick down to the brook, and wet it all over."

So my grandfather took the stick and did as the old man told him. When he came back to the bench, the tinker had a large horn-handled knife open in his hand. With the blade, which seemed very sharp, he made a single cut through the bark of the stick, about a foot from one end, and by holding the knife still, and spinning the stick slowly toward him in his fingers, he carried the cut all the way round. Then, near the end, he cut a deep notch, and four or five smaller notches in a line farther down; and after that he laid the stick across his knee, and turning it all the while, began to pound it gently with the handle of the knife.

When he had pounded a long time, he laid down the knife, and taking the stick in both hands, gave it a little twist. At that, grandfather heard something pop, and saw the bark slip from the end of the stick above the knife-cut, all whole except for the notches, a smooth, green tube.

Of the part of the stick from which he had slipped the bark, the old man cut away more than half, and across the upper end he made a smooth, slanting cut. Then he bade grandfather wet the stick again, and when he had done it, he slipped the bark back to its place, and put the end of the stick in his mouth and began to blow; and out of the holes that he had cut, and which he stopped, one after another, with his fingers, came what grandfather said was the sweetest music he had ever heard — music like the voice of a bird singing a long way off, or like that of a tiny bell.

As the old man played, he seemed to forget all about my grandfather; but by and by he laid down the whistle, and smiled and said, "Come. Now we will make the tree." And together the old man and the boy walked down to the brook, and crossed over on some stepping stones, to a place where the ground was soft and black and wet; and there, while the boy held the stick straight, the old man pushed it far down into the mud until it stood firm and true, with the whistle at the upper end of it. And the old man took off his hat, and bowing to the stick, seemed to my grandfather to make a speech to it.

"Little brother," he said, "we leave you here, where you will never be hungry or thirsty. You have made your little music for us to-day, but when you have grown tall and strong, One Who is greater than I shall play upon you with the breath of His mighty winds; and when this little boy is older than I am now,"—and here he put his hand on my grandfather's head,—"his children's children shall hear your music and be glad."

In a little while after that, the old man put on his pack and went away; but my grandfather could not forget him, and almost every day he looked at the stick by the brook. The whistle at the top began to wither and dry up, and the loose bark cracked open and fell away, until it seemed as if the whole stick must be dead; but one day my grandfather saw that a tiny bud had appeared below where the whistle had been; and the bud became a little sprout, and the sprout a shoot, and other shoots followed, until the stick was indeed a little tree.

Through all the years that came after, it grew taller and stronger, until "The Tinker's Willow" was known as the greatest tree in all the countryside, and the birds did, indeed, build their nests among its branches, and the cattle lay in its shade in the hot noontide.

Even when my grandfather was an old, old man, and had grown-up sons and daughters, and many grandchildren, he loved to sit on the bench by the shop and listen to the voice of the wind among the leaves of the great tree; and then, if we asked him, he would tell us again of the tinker who planted it, and of the music that came from the stick out of which it grew.

THE STORY OF THE LAUREL

Once upon a time there was a great flood over all the earth. Some wicked people had angered the gods, and Jupiter sent all the waters of the earth and sky to cover the earth.

He did not want the waters to dry up until all the people were drowned, so he shut fast in their caverns all the winds except the south wind, which was sometimes called the messenger of the rain. And Jupiter sent this messenger of his to wander over all the earth.

A mighty figure of ruin he was, as he swept along, emptying the clouds as he passed. His face was covered with a veil like the night, his hair was loaded with showers, and his wings and his cloak were dripping wet. The gods of the ocean and the river gods all helped him in his work; till, in a short time the whole earth was out of sight under a vast sea and all the wicked were drowned.

Then Jupiter was sorry to see the earth looking so empty and deserted, so he called home the south wind and set the other winds free. The north wind and the east wind and the gentle west wind swept over the earth until it was again dry and green. After that Jupiter sent a new race of better men and women to live upon it.

But, strange to say, the water had brought forth many queer new animals; and among them was a huge monster, so ugly that I will not even try to tell you what it looked like, and so wicked and cruel that the people for miles around the swampy land where it dwelt lived in constant terror.

No one dared go near the hideous creature until one day, the archer Apollo, the sun-god, came with his glittering arrows, and slew it, after a fierce battle. The people were then very happy. They made a great hero of Apollo, and he left the country feeling very proud of himself.

As he was going along, whom should he meet but the little god Cupid, armed with his bow and arrows. Cupid was the young god of love, sometimes called the god of the bow, and there are many stories about how wonderful his arrows were.

Some of Cupid's arrows were sharp-pointed and made of shining gold, and whoever was pierced by one of these felt love very deeply, at once. But his other arrows were blunt and made of dull lead and, strange as it may seem, made the people whom they struck hate each other.

When Apollo met Cupid thus armed, he began to taunt him.

"What have you to do with the arrow?" he said in a boastful tone. "That is my weapon. I have just proved it by slaying the terrible monster. Come, Cupid, give up the bow which rightfully belongs to me."

Now, Cupid was a very quick tempered little god, and he cried in a passion, "Though your arrow may pierce all other things, my arrow can wound you." Then he flew off in a very bad humor, and tried to think of some way in which he could make Apollo feel which of them was a better marksman.

By and by, he came to a grove in which a beautiful nymph, Daphne, was wandering. This was just what Cupid wanted. He shot an arrow of lead into her heart, and the nymph felt a cold shiver run through her. She looked up to see what had happened, and caught a glimpse of Apollo's golden garments above the tree-tops.

Cupid saw him at the same instant, and, quick as a flash, he planted a golden arrow in Apollo's heart. Then he flew away, satisfied.

The golden arrow did its work only too well. No sooner had the sun-god caught a glimpse of the beautiful nymph, Daphne, than he began to feel a deep love for her. And, just as quickly, Daphne had been made to fear Apollo, and turned and fled from him into the woods.

Apollo followed Daphne in hot haste, calling to her not to be afraid and not to run so fast, for fear she might hurt herself on the thorns and brambles. At last he cried, "Do not try to run from me. I love you, and will do you no harm. I am the great sun-god Apollo!"

But Daphne was only the more terrified at these words and fled more swiftly, while Apollo still pursued her. He had almost reached her side, when she stretched out her arms to her father, the god of the river, along whose banks she was fleeing.

"Oh, father," she cried, "help me! Either let the earth open and swallow me, or so change this form of mine that Apollo will not love me."

Hardly had Daphne finished her plea, when her limbs grew heavy, and a thin bark began to cover her flesh. Her hair changed to green leaves, her arms to slender branches, and her feet, which had borne her along so swiftly, were now rooted to the ground. Her father had answered her plea. Daphne, the nymph, was changed into a laurel tree.

When Apollo saw that his beautiful Daphne had become a tree, he threw his arms about the newly-formed bark and cried, "Since you cannot be my wife, fair Daphne, at least you shall be my tree, my laurel. Your leaves shall be used to crown the heads of the victorious brave, and they shall remain green alike in summer and in winter."

And so it came to pass. The laurel, Apollo's emblem from that day on, became the sign of honor and triumph.

THE LITTLE ACORN

It was a little acorn that hung on the bough of a tree.

It had a tender green cup and a beautifully carved saucer to hold it. The mother oak fed it with sweet sap every day, the birds sang good-night songs above it, and the wind rocked it gently to and fro. The oak leaves made a soft green shade above it, so the sun might not shine too warmly on its green cover, and it was as happy as an acorn could be.

There were many other acorns on the tree, and the mother tree, through her wind voices, whispered loving words to all her babies.

The summer days were so bright and pleasant that the acorn never thought of anything but sunshine and an occasional shower to wash the dust off the leaves. But summer ends, and the autumn days came. The green cup of the acorn turned to a brown cup, and it was well that it grew stiffer and harder, for the cold winds began to blow.

The leaves turned from green to golden brown, and some of them were whisked away by the rough wind. The little acorn began to grow uneasy.

"Isn't it always summer?" it asked.

"Oh, no," whispered the mother oak, "the cold days come and the leaves must go and the acorns too. I must soon lose my babies."

"Oh, I could never leave this kind bough," said the frightened acorn. "I should be lost and forgotten if I were to fall."

So it tried to cling all the closer to its bough; but at last it was alone there. The leaves were blown away, and some of them had made a blanket for the brown acorns lying on the ground.

One night the tree whispered a message to the lonely acorn. "This tree is your home only for a time. This is not your true life.

Your brown shell is only the cover for a living plant, which can never be set free until the hard shell drops away, and that can never happen until you are buried in the ground and wait for the spring to call you. So, let go, little acorn, and fall to the ground, and some day you will wake to a new and glorious life."

The acorn listened and believed, for was not the tree its mother? It bade her good-bye, and, loosing its hold, dropped to the ground.

Then, indeed, it seemed as if the acorn were lost. That night a high wind blew and covered it deep under a heap of oak leaves. The next day a cold wind washed the leaves closer together, and trickling streams from the hillside swept some earth over them. The acorn was buried.

"But I shall wake again," it said, and so it fell asleep. It was very cold, but the frost fairies wove a soft, white snow blanket to cover it, and so it was kept warm.

If you had walked through the woods that winter, you would have said that the acorn was gone. But spring came and called to all the sleeping things underground to waken and come forth. The acorn heard and tried to move, but the brown shell held it fast.

Some raindrops trickled through the ground to moisten the shell, and one day the pushing life within set it free. The brown shell was of no more use and was lost in the ground, but the young plant lived. It heard voices of birds calling it upward. It must grow. "A new and glorious life," the mother oak had said.

"I must arise," the acorn thought, and up the living plant came, up into the world of sunshine and beauty. It looked around. There was the same green moss in the woods; it could hear the same singing brook.

"Now I know that I shall live and grow," it said.

"Yes," rustled the mother oak, "you are now an oak tree. This is your real life."

And the little oak tree was glad, and stretched higher and higher toward the sun.

Milton Keynes UK
Ingram Content Group UK Ltd.
UKHW020657130624
444110UK00011B/350